A LOVE NEVER FORGOTTEN

NEVER FORGOTTEN TRILOGY, BOOK ONE

KALYN COOPER

A Love Never Forgotten

KaLyn Cooper

Cover Artist: Drue Hoffman

Editor: Marci Boudreaux Clark

Published 2018

eBook Published by KaLyn Cooper

Printed in the United States of America

A LETTER TO READERS

Dear Reader,

NOTE: A Love Never Forgotten was originally published as Never Forget, part of the USA Today Bestseller Love Under Siege anthology.

Thank you so much for purchasing A Love Never Forgotten, the first book in the Never trilogy. This book has it all. It falls into the categories of contemporary, military, seasoned romance and romantic suspense, all tied together with a second chance trope.

Although you will meet the entire team that was brought together ten years ago for a single mission that went extremely wrong, A Love Never Forgotten delves into the past, present, and future of Elizabeth Kamp and Mason Sinclair.

Matthew St. Clare has dreamed for months of the gorgeous woman with unique silver eyes, but all too often the beauty of the dream melds into despair in the nightmares. When he meets her, he knows she is the key to his past, present, and hopefully his future.

Elizabeth Kamp just buried her second husband. She

doesn't need another man in her life, but when someone tries to kill her, she'll accept help from a saint to protect her children.

But can she protect her heart from him?

I truly hope you enjoy the story

Always,

KaLyn Cooper

For the latest on works in progress and future releases, check out **KaLyn Cooper's website**

www.KaLynCooper.com http://www.kalyncooper.com/

Follow **KaLyn Cooper on Facebook** for promotions and giveaways https://www.facebook.com/kalyn.cooper.52

Sign up for exclusive promotions and special offers only available in **KaLyn's newsletter** http://www.kalyncooper.com/newsletter.html

I dedicate this book to all those families where both the husband and wife wear military uniforms. The U.S.A. is doubly blessed by you.

ACKNOWLEDGMENTS

Like all my books, A Love Never Forgotten took so many people to bring it to life. I'd like to thank the members of the Black Swan Book Club for all their input. I love the fact they don't hesitate to give me their opinions. The following members assisted in the selection of character names; Denise Poteete, Melissa Marie, Michelle Lambert, Melissa Hultz, Sara Spence Conger, Jessica Whiteway, and Tamara Graham.

My sincere thanks to Marci Clark, my wonderful editor, who made me look at situations from a different angle and rewrite the last two chapters. From the bottom of my heart, I thank my publicist, Drue Hoffman, for pushing my career to new heights.

I thank my husband for putting up with me while I turn this hobby into a career.

CHAPTER ONE

He shouldn't touch her.

But he had to.

Capturing a stray tendril near her temple he wrapped it behind her ear, tracing the outer shell the way she liked it.

Lust filled her steel gray eyes before they turned ice blue and slashed at him in warning. She glanced to the side without moving her head. No one was watching them.

The dream fast forwarded to another place and time.

She attached her dusty camouflage helmet to her backpack then skillfully pulled on a tan stretchy cap covering her gorgeous light brown hair with blond highlights. She tucked in the tight bun at the nape of her neck then ran her fingertips around the edge checking for escaped strands.

You're good. He mouthed the words, so they wouldn't be transmitted over the tiny microphone attached to his ear bud. The two-dozen people monitoring the op could never find out about their personal relationship. Repositioning his hands on his rifle, because damn he wanted to touch her, claim her, let the world know this gorgeous woman was his.

Instead, he swept his gaze over the open dry land. No tangoes. They were safe...for now.

His gaze automatically returned to her.

She extracted the familiar white cloth from an outer pocket of her pack and unfurled the entire eight feet. In seconds she expertly wrapped the pashmina over her head, around her neck then draped the ends over her beautiful breasts, and rank insignia, as though she had been donning a hijab all her life.

"Be careful out there, lieutenant." The voice with the distinct Texas drawl wasn't his, yet he'd said the words. He'd meant them, too. They were in hostile territory, and he couldn't imagine what he'd do if anything happened to her. Probably kill every son of a bitch in that village then burn it to the ground.

She flashed him a bright white smile that touched his heart. "Not my first rodeo, cowboy."

"At the first sign of trouble, we're bugging out." Even a hint that something was wrong, and he'd pull the whole team out of the small Middle Eastern town.

She raised a perfectly arched eyebrow and gave him a *no shit Sherlock* expression, but what she said was, "Yes sir, captain." She glanced over her shoulder to where two other women were covering their hair with similar headdresses.

He checked the seven members of his Special Forces team. All were hyperaware of their surroundings, weapons at the ready.

The stunning woman returned those unique silver-gray eyes with flecks of sky blue to his and she mouthed *I love you.*

His heart flipped over, vowing he'd hear those words again and again. He couldn't lose her. He wouldn't allow anyone to take her from him. They had an entire future planned together.

Turning, she signaled to the other women, and they disappeared over the rise toward another Iraqi village.

His dream wandered on to a more pleasant scene where those same crystalline eyes now sparkled blue with passion as they both panted with need.

Lips, reddened with his kisses, begged him. "In me. Now."

He felt the muscles on the sides of his mouth tighten as he smiled and rolled on top of her. Her legs were spread wide, gripping his hips with strong thighs as he slid bareback into her.

"I love you," she whispered in his ear as he pushed all the way to the hilt. The feel of her hot and wet around him, gripping his cock, knowing she was his, completed him in a way he'd never felt before. He withdrew, ready to pump in again.

She was gone.

Unbelievable fear shot through him as he stretched his hand out for her. The soft sheets of their bed were no longer underneath his palm and fingertips. Rough wooden boards scraped layers off his skin as he reached for her, frantically searching for his woman. He lifted his head off the uneven floor and was introduced to a physical pain unlike anything he'd experienced in his ten years in combat and training.

Door.

He had to get out of there.

He didn't know why, but with his head pounding and his body aching, he crawled through the dark room toward the sliver of light coming from underneath the door. He used every ounce of energy he had trying not to move his head because the searing pain made him want to throw up.

He threw up anyway.

He had to move fast. Extending his arm introduced him to a new level of pulsing agony.

Blood trickled down into both eyes. He wiped it away with the sleeve of his desert camouflage uniform.

Somehow, he'd made it outside. His fingers were raw from crawling through hard packed sand.

Boom.

Boom, boom, boom.

The impact of the explosion forced his entire body into the gritty earth. He couldn't breathe dirt, so he rolled over, gasping to fill his lungs with air.

The sky darkened with falling debris and billowing black smoke.

Large dark chunks hit his legs. He couldn't move them out of the way. His cries of pain were drowned out by the roar of the fire. He tried to lift his arms to shield his face, but the muscles and bones were no longer connected. He jerked to the side, trying to roll, hardly moving an inch.

A large piece of building turned and tumbled its way back to earth, blocking the sun.

Helplessly, he screamed as despair ripped through his body

Matthew St. Clare bolted straight up in bed, still screaming. He gasped, dragging in a much-needed lungful of air. Glancing at the rumpled sheets, he half expected to see a woman, or his legs bloody and mangled. His heart pounded so fast he was drenched in sweat. His thighs and calves ached as though he had just finished a physical fitness test or a strenuous hour of physical therapy.

He controlled his breathing the way he'd been taught as he took in his Potomac Hills, Virginia bedroom. A long mirror ran the length of the wall over a low black dresser with thin silver handles on his right. His bed was a raised platform, the headboard black padded leather attached to the wall. A nightlight in the bathroom was more than enough for

Matt to see he was alone, but he sensed the emptiness of his home.

Grabbing his phone from the nightstand, he checked his security system. Of course, it was all clear. The nightmare had awakened him, nothing else. He slowly inhaled a deep breath through his nose to the count of four and let it out through his mouth counting to eight.

Repeat. Then do it again until your heart doesn't feel like it's trying to burst through your ribs.

He hated the sweet dreams because they always seemed to meld into nightmares. His own mind was betraying him, teasing him with feelings of tenderness and showing him beauty, then catapulting him into the depths of despair.

The visions were happening with increasing frequency, almost every night now.

Perhaps it was the five-year review scheduled to start in a few hours that had him so stressed. Today was supposed to be an easy day, though. He had an early morning appointment to see the psychiatrist. Maybe he should tell the shrink about the woman in his dreams. The mere thought made him chuckle.

Yeah, right. He'll peg me as crazy for sure.

Talking about her would lead to more questions. Hell, he had questions. Matt had never been involved in an explosion, or even near a building while it blew up. He wondered how a psychiatrist would interpret that dream. No, that was a nightmare. His entire body shook from the residual feeling of helplessness. He never wanted to experience that kind of fear, one that went all the way to his core.

No. He'd keep his mouth shut. He didn't want anyone to question whether he was able to handle the job. The job was everything to him. The only thing.

He'd done well at the CIA, moving up regularly. Now, as the deputy director of the Special Activities Division he ran paramilitary officers all over the world. His job was not to set operational goals, but to implement and achieve the mission by providing the men in the field with whatever they needed, whenever they needed it.

He'd started as an implanted local asset in the Middle East then moved up to be an area handler. Thankfully, Gabriel Davis had suggested he apply for an analyst position at headquarters and his mentor had personally recommended him for the job. Matt had followed Gabe up the chain of command. His career had been stellar, both in the field and at Langley, and he had the commendations to prove it. At fifty-two, he wasn't exactly on a fast-track, but at this point in his career, he was happy to be out of fieldwork.

Those missions were better left for the young. Running around the desert and sleeping in makeshift tents, or wherever they could find protection from the heat or cold, was in his past. His car accident had permanently pulled him from fieldwork. He now enjoyed his own soft bed or a five-star hotel if he was on the road.

Giving up on sleep, he crawled out of bed and showered. Wrapped only in a towel resting low on narrow hips, he glanced at the ragged birthmark just inside his right hip. It was small enough no woman ever paid attention to it, but he wondered what it would take to get rid of it. Probably the scar would be worse.

Ignoring the dark brown line, he ran the badger brush under the steaming hot water before dipping it into the mug, vigorously stirring to create shaving lotion. He preferred the old-fashioned glycerin soap and the safety razor to modern foam from a can and a multi-bladed razor.

As he looked at the face in the mirror, for just a second, it was as though a stranger looked back at him. That had happened so often it no longer caught him off guard, but was still disturbing, more so because he couldn't remember the other face a second later.

When his car had been demolished under the tires of an eighteen-wheeler, much of his face had to be reconstructed. His long hair now covered the thin scars next to his hairline that had practically disappeared. He was very thankful for the extremely talented Doctor Jessica Kessler who had rebuilt his face. He appreciated the fact he looked years younger than his chronological age. Multiple surgeries had erased many of the natural aging lines a fifty-two-year-old man should have. If it weren't for his nearly white hair, he would be mistaken for someone in his early forties.

His appearance had served him well when it came to women. He never had a problem finding a bed partner and most were shocked at his physique and stamina. He'd gutted his way through physical therapy to regain the strength in his arms and legs after they'd been broken in nine places. He continued to spend an hour or more every day in the gym to maintain the body he'd worked so hard to remake.

As he scraped away his stubble, he examined his mostly black mustache. It was a vanity point, one of the things that tied him to his previous life where men wore long beards as a sign of virility.

Matt thought about the dream and decided it was nothing more than his overactive brain. Certainly, it wasn't a memory because he'd never met a woman with crystalline blue eyes, or were they gray? A woman like her was definitely memorable. He didn't want some shrink telling him that secretly he wanted to fall in love. In his line of work, a wife, and worse yet, children, were little more than targets for kidnapping. He didn't need the hassle of a wife or kids. As he had risen in the CIA, he realized that when he needed sex, he could have it anytime he wanted.

Maybe that was the problem, he needed to get laid.

Jessica popped into his mind. She would be coming in to reevaluate her work later in the week, even though his physical was scheduled for tomorrow. They had been lovers for a time while he'd still been in physical therapy, but he'd soon grown tired of being the prize pony in her show. She hadn't wanted him for the man he was underneath her exquisite surgical skills, but as a model displaying her capabilities. She'd often told her colleagues that he had deserved the face of an angel since he'd saved so many lives in the Middle East, and she just *had* to give it to him.

Yeah, she'd given it to him all right. He'd fucked her every way he wanted. She'd do anything to him and for him as long as he'd be at her side during hospital and professional functions. He'd needed that reassurance too, though. She made him feel like a man again, at least until he realized he would never be anything more than her last successful project. Their parting of ways had been amicable since she had scored a high-paying job with a Bel Air, California trot surgery clinic, and he was returning to duty at Langley.

That was it. He needed to fuck Jessica. He'd convince her, that a few hours in bed was an excellent way of examining her tiny stitch work. She'd get an up close and very personal view of her painstaking bone reconstruction. Yes. He was convinced his former lover was the solution.

He'd take her from behind. She'd always liked it that way, and in his mind, he'd picture the luscious curves of the woman in his dreams as he pushed into her until they both exploded in ecstasy.

Matt glanced down at the tented towel knowing it wasn't thoughts of Jessica that had aroused him, but the idea of burying himself deep inside the mystery woman. It only took a few strokes of his fist, and the flash of blue gray eyes in his mind to take care of the situation.

An hour later, as he crossed the lobby at headquarters, he

glanced down at the inlaid seal of the Central Intelligence Agency. He always thought it was ironic that even the symbol was in shades of gray rather than black and white, thus lacking any color at all. At this hour of the morning, hundreds of people were entering the sprawling building to begin their work day. His team worked around the clock, so the night crew was about to be replaced by fresh-minded agents.

When he caught a vague whiff of something sweet and spicy, transparent gray eyes with blue flecks flashed through his mind. He immediately searched the crowded room for softly cascading light brown hair with streaks of gold. Several women met the initial criteria but somehow, he knew none of them was the right person. He stood frozen as men and women moved swiftly around him. The scent was gone as quickly as it had registered.

A young man in a gray suit with his cell phone glued to his ear bumped his shoulder from behind. “Sorry, sir.”

Matt growled. “No cell phone use in this area,” he snapped. He glanced at the checkpoint thirty feet ahead. Technically, the twenty-something could use the phone until he reached the bins at the end of the conveyor belt.

“I’ve got to go, sweetie. Daddy’s very proud of you. I’ll see you…” The much younger man walked slowly and took his place in line. He hung up with a contented smile on his face, then placed his phone and keys in a small bowl on the moving black belt.

An unusual pang of guilt hit Matt’s heart. That kid had a kid. Damn. He felt old. But the guy seemed happy about talking with his child. What would that be like?

Terror. He answered his own question. He’d never spent much time around children. As an only child, it wasn’t like he’d taken care of younger siblings or been forced to babysit the neighbor’s kids. Growing up, the nearest neighbor had been three miles away. An immediate picture of a struggling ranch in Wyoming popped into his head. The wind-worn clapboard that had needed painting a decade before was surrounded by sunburned grass, eaten short by bony cattle. He was so thankful that when his parents had been killed, the ranch was sold for taxes. One less thing he had to worry about. He was free of that God-forsaken place.

He tried to mentally pull up a picture of his parents and couldn't. He rubbed his temples where a migraine threatened to start. He knew the best way to avoid the oncoming pain was to bury himself in his work.

Walking past the long line, he swiped his card at the far-left entrance, only glancing at the uniformed guard and the hidden facial recognition camera. He strode to a bank of elevators empty of a crowd. Swiping his badge again, the doors opened. Compared to the barrage of echoing voices in the lobby, the car was blissfully silent as he dropped down to sublevel four.

Matt's body relaxed as he stepped into the darkened theater-style room at the uppermost level. The large screen in front currently showed twenty-six active operations with problems. Desks, containing at least two screens each, filled the five terraced levels. Low voices murmured as the crews turned over the operations. Thank God the noise dampening was top of the line in this room.

As he started to sit in the command post, Justin approached from the side. "Don't get comfortable. Your appointment with the shrink has been changed to right now."

"What the fuck?" Matt hadn't had enough coffee to face the psychiatrist yet.

"Check your email. It's probably all part of the evaluation." Justin sipped his huge container of cola. "You know, can you roll with changes? Are you good at last minute orders?" He spun the executive chair around to face him and slid into the seat. "Like we don't fucking do that every minute of our job. And did they consider *me* when the powers-to-be decided to fuck with your day? Of course not. I was supposed to meet my wife for breakfast at the Willard Hotel to start the celebration of our one-year anniversary as we try to make a baby. But no. They don't care about that."

Slapping his co-worker on the shoulder, Matt decided his day could be worse. "I'm sorry they fucked you over like this. Gabe was going to cover for me."

"He's in with the director of operations this morning." Justin tapped his ear and spoke through the thin communication wire an inch from his mouth to someone on the floor. Pressing buttons, he enlarged the map of Africa, so it filled one quarter of the screen. Live feed of a riot occupied the box. He started snapping out orders.

"I'll be back as soon as I can," Matt promised. He'd keep this meeting as short as possible.

CHAPTER TWO

Elizabeth Kamp pressed her foot on the spongy brake of the aging van she'd purchased just before leaving the Army seven years ago. The line of vehicles had moved a grand total of twenty feet that time. Checking her watch, she congratulated herself for anticipating this kind of traffic.

She never liked going into CIA headquarters at Langley. She much preferred her small, non-descript building in the outskirts of D.C. Her office was closer to home which made it convenient to take both her children to school and pick them up.

After *serious fourth grade work,* as Austin called it, he walked the short block to Liza's daycare, which also offered an outstanding after-school program. Tutoring in reading had been added to her son's daily routine since his last report card, at an expense that stretched their budget even thinner. She'd do anything for her children, even if it meant packing her lunch and making pasta for supper most nights when Robert was working late. Her husband always expected a complete meal from salad, that had better be more than a wedge of lettuce, through a hunk of meat that would feed her and both children, fresh vegetables, potatoes rather than rice or couscous, and a homemade dessert.

She sighed and wondered where her paycheck went. It wasn't like she could work overtime for extra money. She was salaried. Nor could she work harder for more sales like Robert, who seemed to put in increasingly more hours without a proportional growth in income. Truth be told, she didn't mind that he wasn't around much these days.

Pulling into the parking lot, she checked her watch one more time. Her morning was running well. Neither child had spilled anything at breakfast requiring a complete change of clothes, for her or the child. Austin had remembered to put his nightly reading book into his backpack, and Liza actually liked the clothes she picked out the night before. So far, so good.

Because she rarely came to this location, Elizabeth's designated parking area was nearly a mile from the meeting location. There wouldn't be any problem getting in her five thousand steps that day. Since she was walking in high heels, the standard two-inch pumps just like she'd worn for years as a U.S. Army officer, she decided that every step should count as two.

As she crossed the parking lot staring up at the sprawling campus, she took in the original five-story white buildings that seemed to intersect in strange places. It didn't create any distinguishable shape, maybe a blockish letter C in a serif typestyle because it had wings off of wings. Two newer buildings towered over either side of a long flat structure that was the official entrance. The impenetrable green glass always looked eerie to Elizabeth. She thought for a covert agency, the campus was a little over the top.

First, everyone in the world knew exactly where it was. Any country with a spy satellite could figure out how many people worked there by counting the cars in the very exposed parking lot or the number that entered the multi-layered garage. She suddenly felt like looking toward the sky and waving. Certainly someone was watching her long trek to the building. She'd seen satellite photos that could identify the date on a dime lost on a shopping center sidewalk. They wouldn't have any problem figuring out who she was, as long as they had the same facial recognition software and data base located inside the edifice in front of her.

Someone in security had probably already clocked her as a new face on one of the hundreds of cameras secretly located throughout the 258 acres. Access to these offices was considerably easier than a stranger trying to enter her building. That was no surprise. She dealt with top secret conversations, often in real time, happening half a world away. Her specialty was several Arabic dialects.

Elizabeth hoped to breeze through the checkpoint since she didn't have time today to be grilled by someone with a shiny new badge. Although she considered Gabriel Davis a longtime friend as well as mentor, he had no patience for meeting interruptions because someone thought they were more important than him and arrived late. For the former military man, that meant being seated five minutes early.

She'd been called in that day, not to brief on some significant activity in the last twelve hours, but on a specific person of continued interest to the United States. The man she blamed for her first husband's death ten years ago. Nassar al Jamil had been building his army throughout the Middle East before Elizabeth and her new husband, Mason, had gone on that disastrous mission.

Shaking off the sadness that always crept in when she thought about that day and losing the man she had loved, she strode toward the designated briefing room.

Even though Mason had been killed, literally blown to bits with barely enough DNA left to identify him, the mission had been deemed successful. The local CIA asset had come through with accurate intelligence. The U.S.A. had proven that Russia had been supporting al Jamil in creating his version of the New Islamic State, placing himself in charge as Allah's representative on earth. The terrorist wanted an entire new country carved out of existing nations, dedicated to fundamentalist Islamic beliefs. During the past ten years, the self-proclaimed Caliphate had been working diligently toward that goal, getting closer every day as his hatred for Western ways grew exponentially.

Elizabeth wanted Nassar al Jamil dead. Mason's death was the first and foremost.

As a modern female, born and raised in the United States, the man stood for everything she despised. While stationed in Afghanistan and Iraq, she'd spent time working with women who had been beaten within an inch of their lives simply for not having food on the table when their husband arrived home…even though there was nothing in the hovel to eat and she certainly hadn't been given money to shop for food.

She had once held a frightened twelve-year-old in her arms, assisting in the birth of a baby as the men in the village laughed outside the shed door. Upon the first tiny cry, her husband, old enough to be her grandfather, rushed in. When he'd discovered the newest addition to the family was female, he'd smacked the pre-teen across the face and threatened her that next time she'd better give him a boy. He'd sold his newest daughter's virginity through an arranged marriage before they were out of earshot. The idiot would never understand that the sperm determined the sex of the child, not the mother. She'd been told that Middle Eastern men would consider the scientific fact nothing more than another Western lie.

Very little good had happened to women throughout her

tours in the Middle East. Occasionally, she'd find an enclave where the men were more progressive, but the basic fundamentalist beliefs—especially polygamy and consummating a marriage as soon as a young girl had her first period, so she could breed—had always baffled her. There was no reason, in this day and age, to marry simply for the purpose of procreation. The world had more than enough hungry mouths to feed. And what about love? That emotion was not included in the beliefs of men like al Jamil.

In her world, love was essential to marriage. Her parents weren't perfect, by any means, but they loved each other and all their children. They took turns parenting. She had fond memories of time alone with each parent as well as both with just her. Of course, they also did many things as a family. Elizabeth had wanted to make the same kind of home for her family. Life just hadn't worked out that way, though. She loved both Austin and Liza with all her heart, gave each *mommy time*. To her disappointment, Robert claimed he wasn't the nurturing kind of father.

In her opinion, he was the mostly the absent kind.

She'd thought a lot lately about how she was raising her two children practically alone…and always had. When Liza had croup as an infant, her husband wouldn't even take care of his stepson for an hour while she took their baby to the doctor. Robert had never developed a relationship with Austin and she was tired of playing peacekeeper between the two of them. She could raise her son and daughter by herself. That very morning had proven she could juggle two children, a house, and a full-time job without a husband.

Besides, she'd never had any help from the beginning, so caring for her children alone was nothing new. Austin had been conceived on her wedding night to Mason. Six weeks after the devastation of losing her new husband, she discovered she was pregnant. Thrilled that she would have a piece of his love with her forever, Elizabeth had taken joy in being a single parent and an active duty Army officer. Then she had moved on, left the Army, and eventually created a new life with Robert.

They had created this beautiful little girl who meant the world to Elizabeth. After her birth, though, she and Robert seemed to drift apart. Did she really want a divorce?

Rounding the final corner, she refused to dwell on her personal situation and tried to refocus on al Jamil and his antiquated values. Scoffing, she had a fleeting final thought of the similarities between the terrorist and her own husband.

As she walked into the conference room, she smiled at her old friend, Gabriel Davis. He'd been in charge of the fateful mission where she'd lost Mason. Well, in charge on site. Of course, he'd taken orders from someone back at Langley. But Gabe ran the op in Syria, handling his local asset who had reported the location of the Russian guns and ammunition. Their on-site photos had appeared in newspapers around the world and were now part of an official congressional transcript.

In those first terrifying minutes after the force of the explosion knocked her on her ass, she had run toward the burning building. Gabe had caught her and thrown her over his shoulder, literally kicking and screaming, and then dragged her out of the country. Her behavior could definitely be classified as unbecoming of an Army officer. That night, with dirt from the explosion still covering her entire body, she hadn't cared if Gabe had turned her in.

Mason was gone.

When Austin was nearly two, Elizabeth had confided in Gabe that she was seriously considering leaving the military. He had found her the awesome job she still had. All day she listened to Arabic conversations. Her job was to identify whether that person was a current or future threat, or someone spouting off wanting to look like the biggest cock on the block. Then she had to determine if he was truly a threat to the tentative peace so many Americans had fought and died for, including Mason.

"Elizabeth, thank you so much for driving in today." The ruggedly handsome man in his late forties glanced up from the papers strewn on the table in front of him and gave her a small smile. "Your insight in this situation is always valued." He laid his hands flat on the table. "I know you still have an emotional connection when it comes to Nassar al Jamil, but I'm extremely proud of the way you can set that aside to do your job."

"Thank you." She glanced at the faces around the room that had suddenly become silent. Some were familiar while others were new, and she understood why Gabe had announced his support the moment she'd entered. Obviously, someone seated at the table had questioned her ability to detach and analyze. Once again, she was grateful he was on her side.

Elizabeth made her way around the conference table, smiling at some and nodding to others as she passed, to take her seat beside him. She wondered how Gabe would take the latest news about their old nemesis. Unfortunately, she'd be the bearer of bad news.

She laid her briefing folder on the table and sat down in the comfortable chair to his right. She glanced at the file stamped top secret before she met his eyes. Quietly she asked, "Do you already know what's in here?"

"Not exactly, but I have a pretty good idea." Gabe pulled a spreadsheet from the pile and slid it over to her. "We'll get to this eventually, but I want you to brief us first."

She nodded and followed his gaze to the clock just above the door. As the big hand moved to the top of the hour, Gabe announced, "We'll now get started." After the usual preliminaries, he called on her.

"Nassar al Jamil is once again on the move." She clicked a button on the remote in her hand and a map of the Middle East appeared on the large flat screen. It zoomed in on the area from the Persian Gulf to the Caspian Sea which included Iran, Iraq, Syria, and Turkey. "In a conversation he had seventeen hours ago with Abdul Sayyed, one of the most trusted advisors to the president of Iran, al Jamil was given permission to move his followers to Lake Urmia in the north western corner that borders Iraq and Turkey and is less than one hundred miles from Syria. We already know he has a very strong base in the eastern most triangle of that country." With a laser pointer, she indicated the two hundred square miles of Syria that seemed to jut into Iraq.

Then she used the bright red dot to circle Mosul. "This has been one of the most contentious areas throughout the Iraqi war. Al Jamil's half-brother, Turhan, controls that area, but don't get too excited because he has nearly fifty siblings, twenty-eight are brothers. Not all of them believe he is the caliphate. Fact is, most of them think he's full of shit, especially when he hits them up for money." She internally snickered at several of the conversations she had interpreted. She would go as far as to say that most of his brothers thought of him as little more than a zealot preaching to preserve a way of life that ended a millennial before Mohamed was even born.

"Speaking of money." Elizabeth turned her head to look at Gabriel for direction. When he nodded his head, she continued. "Al Jamil has always been well-funded." She looked to the end of the table where several new faces sat together. Without asking permission, and not knowing the backgrounds of the newbies, she decided to explain. "Nassar al Jamil is very much like Osama bin Laden. Both had billionaire fathers and were too far down the list of children to inherit much of anything. According to our psychological analysts they both suffer from Middle Child Syndrome, and through charisma and cunning have built an empire."

Turning back to the screen and pointing the laser at the brownish colored lake on the satellite photo, she announced, "And now he and his followers have found a home. He has never backed off the claim that he was chosen by Allah to create a country that follows the ways of what he calls the true men of Allah."

Elizabeth took a moment to look at each face around the table, finally landing on Gabriel. She reached into her classified folder and passed out the translation from al Jamil's conversation with Abdul Sayyed. Without giving any one an opportunity to read, she pushed on. "According to this conversation, the president of Iran, through al Jamil, is ready to pick up where Osama bin Laden left off. This also confirms what we had thought for some time, Iran had financially supported al Qaeda."

She took a sip of water. "Earlier, I called the leader of Iran the president. That is not the term that he, and those who live within that country's borders, uses to refer to him. Technically, he is the Supreme Leader of Iran and thus is the leader of the Islamic Revolution." She held up the translation. "It seems he is now ready to take on the world, especially the United States of America."

With the click of a button, the transcript appeared on the screen. Scrolling through to the second page, she used the pointer to underscore the words *tip of Allah's sword*. "And they are using al Jamil as their international army."

"Or scape goat when it all goes to shit."

Since everyone at that end of the table had their heads down taking notes, Elizabeth had no idea who had made the comment. Several snickered.

"You are absolutely right," she confirmed. Several gazes met hers. "What this does is officially put Nasser al Jamil on the CIA list of most wanted." There. She'd said it. That was her official recommendation. Having thousands of agents hunting him had been her goal for over ten years.

"Whoa." Gabriel warned from the seat next to hers. "Let's not jump there just yet."

She whirled to face him. "We've put men on the Most Wanted List for less. You see those translations. We've been watching him for over ten years. He has progressively escalated and now has the backing of an enemy of the United States. Are you suggesting we sit back and do nothing but continue watching?"

"He has family living in the United States." Gabe met her glare with one of his own. "There is no direct threat to the U.S. that could be deemed clear and present danger. Hell, Elizabeth, there's nothing here except generalizations."

"I can name ten men on that list that we have even less proof of probable threat, yet they are considered one of the most dangerous men in the world." She took a deep breath and reined in her emotions. She had held them in check thus far, but they were beating down the gate. "I'm not asking that al Jamil bobble to the top ten, I'm only asking that he be placed on the list."

Gabriel stared up at her for a long a minute. "You know that I have to run this past the director of operations before I can even submit it." There was a tightening around his eyes that made her doubt the request would go beyond the next step up the ladder.

"I'm aware this has a long way to go before we send a SOG team after him." Elizabeth wished she had the power to send men from the Special Operations Group after al Jamil immediately, but without a presidential okay, that was impossible.

Gabe chuckled. "We're nowhere near that point yet. I am, though, going to forward this request with a strong recommendation that we put additional assets in place and increase phone taps." He gave her sheepish grin. "That means more work for you, you know."

"I don't mind as long as we nail this bastard." To soften her statement, she added, "Eventually."

"Let's see what else we have to strengthen the request." As Gabriel went through each report, there was very little to add that would point the finger at al Jamil until it came to the financial report.

"I see a significant increase in funds coming from his Caribbean accounts." Gabe looked up expectantly at Steve Gaylord.

The bald man smiled showing dingy yellow teeth. "Before we go any further, I want you all to meet Martha Cables. She'll be taking over for me starting next week." With a huge smile, he announced, "I'm retiring." After a round of applause, and congratulations, they got down to the spreadsheet.

"I've changed the layout slightly." Martha put the spreadsheet onto the big screen. "We're damn good at following money, in both directions, but most of what you see on television is bull. What you have in front of you shows what we have tracked, what we can track, but you'll notice the largest section is what we aren't able to follow. This money can be coming from anywhere. Given the electronic traffic between al Jamil's accounts and the countries that used to be part of the Soviet bloc, and it looks to us as though Russia is filtering him money. Most likely that is to pay for the arms and ammunition purchases we were told about earlier in this briefing. Supplying an army is expensive and you can see from this spreadsheet that he's getting the money to pay for it."

Elizabeth was deep into the line items and huge numbers hoping she could mentally cross reference anything, even the most minute detail, with the conversations she frequently heard. "There are tens of millions of dollars here and we have no way of knowing where that money came from."

When the room turned quiet, she looked up. Well, damn. She must have said that out loud.

Martha's back immediately went straight. "We do the absolute best we can with the resources that we have."

"No, please." Elizabeth smiled at the woman who seem to be about her same age. "I'm just mentally scrolling through the list of his relatives living here in the United States. Is there a way to tell where the transfers originate? Perhaps geographically?"

At this new idea, Martha stilled then glanced toward Steve. "There might be a way we could look at electronic transfers through one of the feds. Billions of dollars run through every day, usually from one Federal Reserve Bank to another. Small amounts are sent to cover purchases by visitors traveling in the Caribbean. If we had any idea what day and which Federal Reserve Bank they were using, we might, and I'm only saying might, be able to track it back to a personal or corporate checking account."

"That's a whole lot of ifs." Gabe pointedly looked at the clock above the door. "Martha, if you get that system worked out, be sure to tell me. In the meantime, keep up the good work. Steve, it was a pleasure working with you. Enjoy your retirement. Elizabeth, I'll do what I can, but please be patient." He glanced around the table then stood. "Thank you all for coming." Everyone in the room knew a dismissal when they heard it.

As the room cleared, Gabriel seemed to watch her. "We'll get him. It's just going to take more time."

She held his gaze. "I'm going to make sure we get him."

CHAPTER THREE

"Well, tell me, Matthew, overall how has it been going for you?" Dr. Sydney Petersen flipped through the inch-thick file with part of Matt's social security number on the tab.

"I don't have any complaints." It was the truth. Certainly, none he was going to share with the agency psychiatrist. His job appeased his need for adrenaline. His off-duty hours were filled with workouts in the gym in an adjoining building, beers with fellow agents, and women whenever he wanted one. Life was good.

"It looks as though you've moved up steadily in the agency. We're very proud of you for doing that." He paused and read for a minute. "Hmm. It looks like you were having nightmares during your last review, but that was five years ago. And I see we got you into our sleep study center." He held up the next page. "Ah. Yes. The electroencephalogram showed you had a great deal of brain activity during sleep, but I can see from the polysomnography that it wasn't physical discomfort causing your light state of sleep." He then looked up.

Matt simply stared back at him. There wasn't a question in there that needed answering.

"Often after a severe accident like yours, the body can't get comfortable which results in restless sleep." The psychiatrist hadn't said anything Matt didn't already know, so he let the man in his mid-sixties talk. "Not the case with you, although I'm sure you still experience stiffness in the shoulder and chest. Oh, and the legs where they were broken. Physically, you've made a remarkable recovery. Any more nightmares?"

Matt made an instant decision not to mention the vivid, disturbing dreams. Since they weren't memories, because none of that shit happened to him, were they premonitions? And who the fuck would believe him if he started being able to tell the future? Had his multiple head surgeries triggered a part of his brain that could predict outcomes? Or were they just his imagination running wild? Why did he get emotionally involved in the scenes? And why was it always the same woman? He needed to research that subject, privately, on a computer where no one, especially the CIA, could track his inquiries.

"No. Not anymore." He lied with the ease of a trained operative. The image of stunning silver eyes opening sleepily next to him brought a smile to his face. To cover his reaction, he admitted, "Unless you call dreaming of a gorgeous brunette waking up next to me, begging me to fuck her again, a nightmare." His smile broadened. "Oh, but those are day dreams, too." He hoped he'd covered his falsehood.

"Since you brought it up, how is your sex life?" The shrink stared at him with interest.

Matt shrugged. "Fine, for a man my age, I guess." Then he qualified, "How many fifty-two-year-olds can still get it up three times a night without the help of a little pill?" He proudly straightened in the leather seat and gave the other man a cocky smile. "Not to brag, but I wore out that cute little barista in the coffee shop downstairs a few weeks ago."

"Are you dating her?" The man across the desk raised an eyebrow.

"Fuck, no." Matt relaxed back into the chair. "We talked sometimes, especially when I was working late. She came on to me. I took her up on her offer. We both knew it was a one-night thing." He stared into the older man's hazel eyes before he admitted. "Besides, I figured she was a plant, testing me for this eval. Not a coincidence she found another job shortly after we spent the night together, was it?"

The corners of the physician's mouth twitched before he pressed on. "She was rather young for you. Are you looking for a younger woman? Maybe one who can give you a few children?"

He didn't want any kids. Never had. "I'm not looking for any woman on a permanent basis. My position here with the CIA precludes any kind of a long-lasting relationship. I've watched coworkers be torn apart when their wife took the kids and left them because of the long hours and the secrets we're not allowed to share. Our work is too important. An agent can't leave the job just because his kid is sick at school and it's his week to play father."

"That's a really good attitude." The doctor's compliment surprised Matt even more when he added, "I'm glad you've come to that decision." As though he'd ever wanted a family with a wife waiting at home with a hot supper and two attention-demanding kids. No fucking way.

An hour later, muscles stiff from sitting in the chair far too long, Matt walked out of the doctor's office and into the open area where the secretary usually sat. Suddenly, a door on his right opened. He couldn't help but look in at the man in the hospital bed, IVs in his arms, as he stared motionless at the television on the ceiling. Headphones covered his ears. With a blocking out sound or feeding him words?

In his head, Matt could hear a soothing male voice talking to him. He couldn't understand what was being said but he was sure someone had spoken. Unease filled him.

Glancing around the open space, he saw no one.

His gaze returned to the hospital-like room seen only through an eight-inch crack in the door. The heart monitor drew white squiggly lines that jumped as the secretary spoke to the man in a white lab coat on the other side of the room. "Dr. Petersen wants you to run him through the process again to be sure everything is solidly embedded."

"I know what I'm doing. This isn't my first time. Not even my twenty-first block." When the man looked up from his tablet, he stared beyond the woman, directly at Matt.

She spun around to face him and pasted on a smile. "Senior Special Agent St. Clare, is there something I can do to help you?"

At the footsteps approaching behind him, Matt turned to see Dr. Petersen. "Matthew, have you seen our new relaxation room? Do you remember napping in the old one when we were located in the other wing?"

"No." Then corrected himself. "Maybe." The anxiousness intensified into full blown dread.

With a gentle hand on his shoulder, the doctor effectively turned him toward the exit while the secretary had discreetly closed the door and slid into the chair behind her desk. "We understand the stress of this job. Sometimes what we do here can cause physical pressure, as well as emotional anxiety, and we just need a little downtime. Many of our executives take advantage of our relaxation and rejuvenation facility."

Even though the doctor made it sound like a fucking spa, deep inside his brain he knew better. Matt needed to get the hell out of there. Fast. "Thanks for the offer, doc, but I'm good."

The psychiatrist squeezed his shoulder and slowed his steps. "When you first came back to us from the Middle East, do you remember having difficulty readjusting to the American way of life? You'd been undercover for so long that the abundance available in the United States and the fast pace of life had you on edge. You spent some time in a room very similar to that one. We had a different facilitator back then. Do you remember Sam Blaylock?" The psychiatrist's chuckle sounded forced.

He didn't give Matt a chance to answer before he continued. "That's okay. It was a long time ago. We've made several changes to the process since then."

When they reached the door, the doctor held the handle, effectively blocking Matt's escape. "Any time you feel this job is getting to be too much for you, the facility is open twenty-four-seven. We also now offer acupuncture and massage therapy which might give you a few hours relief from any pain remaining from your accident."

"Will it help with headaches?" Damn it. Matt had decided he wouldn't mention the headaches.

The psychiatrist glanced up his eyebrows pinched. "What kind of pain are you having?"

Matt instantly knew he was in trouble. "Nothing big. I'm sure it's just stress from looking at the screens for hours on end." To emphasize his point, he rubbed his eyes.

The doctor's facial expression relaxed. "Eye stress is quite understandable. You should talk to the physician about it tomorrow during your physical exam."

"I'll do that." He then grinned. "I might take you up on the massage therapy if there are beautiful women willing to rub my naked body. Do they guarantee a happy ending like the Asian Moon Massage Palace next to the interstate?"

The doctor laughed out loud and shook his head. "The masseuse at night is Sven, and he is excellent at deep tissue massage, but I don't think he'd give you the kind of happy ending you're looking for since your record still indicates that you prefer women. Sven is bisexual, though."

Matt grinned. "I'm glad they got that part right."

He turned to leave but Dr. Petersen caught him by the elbow this time. "If you ever want to talk, call my assistant for an appointment. The higher you move up in the agency, the more I am available to you."

"I'll remember that." He pushed the door open forcing the psychiatrist to release his hold.

As Matt fled down the hall, he wondered if he should tell the doctor about the woman in his dreams. They were there to help employees like him. Men who had seen too much, done things in the name of the United States that conflicted with their own morals, endured constant high stress situations. If Dr. Petersen could make the nightmares go away, it might be worth his confession. He turned and walked back into the office. Noting that the receptionist was gone again, Matt headed toward Dr. Petersen's door which stood open. The doctor was talking but he couldn't see anyone in the room. Perhaps he was dictating or maybe he was talking on the phone.

"Sir, we may have a problem." Concern was woven into every word.

That grabbed Matt's attention.

"He is showing signs that his memory may be coming back. We might need to reprogram him again."

Reprogram? Again? Matt's gaze flew to the closed door of the hospital style room. There had always been rumors about brainwashing, but Matt had considered the idea to be too Hollywood to be real.

There was a long pause before the doctor obediently said, "Yes, sir." Another pause.

"But, sir." The doctor rushed on to say, "I don't believe we need to go to that drastic length." Defensively, Dr. Petersen added, "Our techniques have improved considerably in the last ten years." Pause. "Yes. I agree. The last thing we want is for his memory to return until we're ready."

Ten years. Was the psychiatrist talking about the man in the bed...or him? Matthew was stunned. He couldn't process everything he'd heard. He stood frozen in place, eavesdropping through the slightly open door. So many questions raced through his mind.

The side door to the relaxation clinic started to open, then abruptly closed, bringing him out of his immobility. He made a quick dash for the front door, shoving it closed behind him as he heard the secretary talking as she exited the sterile-looking room once again.

Fuck. That was too close. Matt's heart rate was nearing one hundred fifty beats per minute according to his high-tech watch. He slowed his pace but lengthened his stride to look casual as he put distance between himself and the psychiatrist's office. He needed to get a grip. He needed to get back to work and make sure it appeared as though nothing had changed.

But everything was now different.

As Matt strode down the hall toward the exclusive elevators for the sub levels, he saw his boss, Gabriel Davis, walking and chatting with a woman twenty feet ahead. Her professional navy-blue business suit screamed agent. The way she comfortably walked in two-inch heels told him she had worn them for years. Short cropped light brown hair skimmed the bottom of her collar and curled under in a popular style preferred by many women in the building. Definitely an agent.

The woman had a fantastic ass. The pencil skirt hugged the bottom of her cheeks with every step. She had a slim, athletic build. His favorite kind. She could take anything he offered, even if it got a little rough. Not that he was into kinky, but every now and then he just needed a hard and fast fuck. Some women were just too physically and emotionally fragile for that kind of sex. He didn't think the woman in front of him would have a problem with anything he wanted to do to her or with her.

The casual way the two talked indicated they were very familiar with each other. Briefly, Matt wondered if Gabe was dating her. If so, good for him. If not, maybe he would introduce them.

As they approached the checkpoint in the brightly lit foyer, the two stopped close to the elevators. When the woman turned, she slid on a pair of sunglasses, and spoke briefly to Gabe before nodding and leaving.

Matt had hung back to give them privacy, but he now joined his friend who patiently waited for the elevator doors to open.

"You tap that yet?" Matt stepped beside Gabe and asked quietly enough that the hidden recording devices that were everywhere couldn't hear. They both glanced over as the woman walked through the glass doors into the nearly blinding sunshine.

Gabe's gaze flew to Matt and seemed to study his face. "No. Never. She's an old friend, and I want to keep it that way." His voice was firm and in a natural tone, almost as though he wanted his response recorded.

Friend category. Good to know. Matt's gaze never left the woman until she was out of sight. "How would you feel about introducing me to your friend?" He didn't hide the question.

"Never going to happen." Gabe's grin looked forced. "I want to keep her as my friend."

The doors opened to an empty elevator and they stepped in. The moment of silence broke the feminine distraction and the psychiatrist's words came rushing back like a cold Pacific wave chilling Matt to the bone. He needed to talk to somebody about this.

"Want to grab a beer after work tonight?" he suggested.

"You can buy me all the beer you want, but I'm still not going to introduce you to her." Gabe sighed. "Sorry, but I can't tonight. This is my week with the kids, and I have them *all* this week, by myself."

His friend had three children that Matt knew about. He vaguely remembered Gabe's first wife, but their son was an outstanding athlete. He and Gabe had gone to the boy's high school basketball game a few months ago. The kid could play. He had two little kids with his second wife who had left him within the last year. Matthew was pretty sure reconciliation was never going to happen, but he wasn't positive if they were divorced yet. Official paper or not, his friend had only slept alone when he wanted to.

Needing to sound casual, Matt asked, "How is the college hunt going with...your oldest?" Because damn, he couldn't remember the kid's name.

Gabe beamed. "Guess I hadn't told you yet. Brad got accepted to West Point."

"The Military Academy is an excellent school. He's lucky to be able to go there. When I..." Matthew hesitated. He'd almost said, *when I went there*. But he'd gone to Georgetown and studied political science focusing on Middle Eastern studies, not West Point where military service immediately after graduation was mandatory. Matt had never been in the military.

The picture of a pair of desert camouflage utilities laid out on a cot flashed through his mind. Hands lacing up desert military boots came into focus. The boots were on his feet. That vision was so real Matt glanced down at his highly polished black wingtips.

Pain hit him like a hot needle jabbing into his head just behind his eye.

His hand automatically went to rub his left temple.

Covering for his slip, he lied. "When I was talking with my next-door neighbor the other day—I think you met him, Jim Nelson, he's chief of staff for a congressman from Oregon —he was telling me that he had to review over two hundred applications of high school seniors begging for an appointment to one of the academies."

As they stepped from the elevator and headed the short distance to the Special Activities Division, Gabe told him, "His stepfather owns land in Montana, part of some kind of family farm, but enough to be considered a resident. My ex personally walked Brad in to meet that state's senators and congressmen as soon as he applied, long before the kid ever said he was really interested in going there." Gabe shook his head. "I hope to Christ this is what he really wants. I don't think his mother understands that he'll be going to war within five years. She absolutely hated it when I was deployed. She's going to lose her fucking mind the first time he's sent overseas with a rifle in his hands."

All Matt could do was nod slowly and grunt in agreement, although the pain was quickly dissipating. These weird flashes of pain were coming more often. He'd mention it during his physical tomorrow.

Gabe reached for his office door. "I've got some phone calls to make. I'll meet you inside the command center within an hour." He opened a door and stopped after one step. Turning he gave Matt a reassuring grin. "We'll grab that beer early next week. I'm going to need one by then. Probably two or three."

Once again, Matt was thankful he didn't have either a wife or children.

CHAPTER FOUR

"Abd al Rashid, our time is coming soon." His favorite uncle called him by his Arabic name as he spoke in an unusual Middle Eastern dialect, but the man understood his father's brother perfectly. It was his original language...in the *time before* as he thought of it. Before his parents had been killed by unbelievers. Before he'd ended up in an Iraqi refugee camp with the hundreds of other children. Before the Catholic church sent him to the United States of America. Before his American family had raised him forcing their Christian values on him.

"Uncle, I have been put here to serve Allah. Tell me what you need." The man plucked the Montblanc pen from the marble set on his desk and slid over a pad of paper. He preferred things old school. Modern technology was too traceable, a fact he knew very well. As the list grew, he mentally started calculating costs. Although he wasn't sure of the going price for train loads of lumber, concrete, and other building materials, he had people for that. The excitement in his uncle's voice buoyed his mood. The prophecy was finally coming true. He could literally help build the new world. And would. In the memory of his parents.

Oozing red blood blurred the legal sheet before he blinked away the last mental picture of his parents. Riddled with bullets from American guns, his parents laid side by side, their arms and legs at odd angles. They had died fighting for their beliefs. He would continue the effort.

List complete, he said his good-byes and tucked the encrypted satellite phone back in his pants pocket.

His desk phone rang. After glancing at the caller ID, he grinned with satisfaction. He hit the button to encrypt the call and blank out any listening devices planted in his office, then answered the inner agency line. "Director Davis, I was thinking about you this morning."

"Sir, I have news about an old friend I thought I'd share." He was pleased that Gabriel had followed protocol and had given the right code asking about the security of their line.

"I'm always interested in catching up on old friends," he replied correctly. "I take it we're talking about Senior Special Agent Matthew St. Clare?"

"Yes, sir. I'm afraid he might be getting his memory back." Gabriel confirmed the psychiatrist's earlier concerns. "But maybe not. He didn't recognize Elizabeth."

"When the fuck did he see her?" He straightened his back and glared at the desk unit as though it were his director of Special Activities Division.

"She was here this morning with the latest translations from Nassar al Jamil." Gabriel quickly added, "I sent you the audio yesterday morning before she ever got them."

He'd heard the conversation and did his own translations. He'd known his uncle was going to call hours before he'd answered the special phone. "Did she press you again to put him on the Most Wanted List?"

"Yes, sir." Gabriel chuckled. "I told her I was just the first step, and it had to be pushed up the chain of command. I also told her there wasn't enough immediate threat for that drastic move."

"Good. So, back to Agent St. Clare. When did they meet?" Deftly the man's fingertips flew over keys. He found the conference room where the meeting had taken place as well as the footage of her walking into the building.

"They never actually met," Gabriel explained. "He must've been behind us as I walked her out."

Quickly pulling up the video, he watched Matthew St. Clare walk down the hall, following Gabriel and Elizabeth several feet back. He could tell the instant the agent took notice of a woman. Reassured they never met face to face, he let out a long sigh.

"Thank you for reporting this information. I agree. He doesn't show any recognition of her. What makes you think his memory is returning?" he pressed.

"I was talking about my son getting into West Point. I would swear Matthew almost said something about going to school there. He tried to cover it, but I caught it." The creak of Gabriel's chair gave away his discomfort.

"Good work, Gabriel. Keep an eye on him and keep me informed." Without a good-bye, he hung up the phone. He allowed himself four minutes to watch the video again, examining every facial expression on Agent St. Clare.

He relaxed back in his executive chair, pleased that Davis was so observant and had called him. Keeping information from him was never a good idea. Davis had learned that lesson the hard way back in Syria. His usefulness had always been tentative. He was disposable. As was Elizabeth.

They were two of only five people alive today who might be able to jeopardize his plans. St. Clare could put him in jail for life...if he ever remembered what had happened in Syria ten years ago. If his reprogramming failed, they had options.

If I have to kill them all, I have to kill them all. Everyone dies at some point.

CHAPTER FIVE

Three weeks later

Elizabeth's heels sank into the soft earth under the neatly trimmed grass of the Grandview Cemetery as the pallbearers carried her husband's body to its final resting site. She was so thankful that her mother had driven the three hours from her home near the Blue Ridge Mountains to be there to support her that week. After burying her father two years earlier, her mother was well versed in the business of death and was able to help her handle many of those decisions.

It had been over ten years since Elizabeth had buried Mason, and she'd had the Special Forces Casualty Assistance Officer there to guide her through all the arrangements and the legalities since he'd been an Army officer. For some reason, there seemed to be so many more decisions about burying Robert.

With Liza's small hand in hers, Austin on the other side helping his grandmother, her family followed the funeral director's instructions to the front row of plastic folding chairs covered in white cloth under a well-used tent bearing the logo of the funeral home. Robert's family took up the next two rows. Behind them, several dozen friends and coworkers gathered in small groups.

Her boss and a few of the other translators from her office stood together in the sunshine in silent support of her. They'd never even met Robert, nor had she met any of their spouses. Her office didn't socialize outside of work. Some other CIA friends milled close by but hadn't approached, only made eye contact. None of them had ever met Robert either. Given who they worked for, she didn't consider that unusual.

Robert's boss came to the funeral service at the cathedral, but had made his apologies to her, claiming he was needed back at the office immediately. Four of his coworkers stood talking quietly several feet away, ready to bolt as soon as this portion was over. She didn't recognize any of them, but after Liza had been born, they hadn't attended many functions associated with his work. Looking back, she wasn't sure if that had been Robert's choice or he had just quit asking her to go with him.

Several friends from church huddled together, as did a group of women she'd met for regular play dates for Liza. When she had to work late, and Robert had been on one of his frequent out of town trips, one of those friends would pick up her children and take Liza and Austin to their home. Those women had become her lifeline. They'd often get the children together on summer evenings in someone's yard, allowing the kids to play as they drank wine and complained about busy husbands and their own jobs.

Near the back of the gathering group, two men and a woman stood off to the side. They'd positioned themselves so they could see everything and everyone. Once, they had been her teammates. Now they were her touchstones. She was moved beyond belief that they had all shown up.

She and Teagan Williams talked at least once a week and tried to get together for lunch once a month. The former Seahawk pilot had left the Navy a few months after Elizabeth, but their reasons for leaving the military had been very different. Elizabeth had been facing deployment, again, but Austin was only two years old. A toddler was the last thing her parents needed in their lives. Teagan hung up her uniform to take care of her mother who had been diagnosed at sixty-one with early onset of Alzheimer's disease.

Next to her, Logan Jackson stood straight back, square shouldered and looked like a Marine, whether he was in uniform or the civilian clothes that never seemed to fit his muscled body quite right, like the navy sports jacket over a white shirt he now wore. Elizabeth was surprised he'd made the trip from Camp Lejeune, North Carolina just to be with her that day. She was positive that as commanding officer of Special Operations Command he had men in danger all over the world and had better things to do than stand in silent support of her as she buried a man he had openly disliked.

On Teagan's other side, Navy Commander Micah Reid constantly scanned the crowd as well as every square foot of land as far as the eye could see. Elizabeth worried about her friend who had driven up from Little Creek, Virginia the day before, and had spent several hours with her and her family the previous night. He'd been wonderful with Austin, who had sequestered himself in his bedroom since returning home from school after hearing the news that his stepfather was dead. Micah was about to retire after commanding over one thousand Navy SEALs. He hadn't decided yet what he was going to do, but she knew he lived for the adrenalin rush. So had she, at one time.

These three had helped her through the worst day of her life, and several that immediately followed. Elizabeth's gaze wandered to the headstone two spaces over. Mason A. Sinclair. U.S. Army Special Forces. He'd only been thirty-two years old when the explosive charges went off early with her new husband still inside the munitions dump. Losing him in such a violent way, right in front of her, had sent her over an emotional edge.

A tear escaped her eyes.

Good. Everyone will think it's for Robert.

She'd shed very few tears for his actual death. The week before she'd cried her eyes out for the death of their marriage, her failure as a wife, and as a woman unable to keep a husband sexually satisfied enough to stay monogamous. Elizabeth had discovered that her husband had been having an affair, and this woman wasn't his first, she had hit the roof then bounced to rock bottom. What had upset her more than anything else was that she hadn't seen the signs. She was a trained observer but seemed to leave those skills at the office. She was equally as mad with herself as she was with him. Their marriage should have ended years ago when he started working at the Pennsylvania facility more and more, and spending weekends up there. At least that's where he said he was.

She'd accepted her loss of Robert eleven days ago. When the D.C. police had called informing her that he'd been in an accident, asking her to go to an unfamiliar hospital, miles away, it had seemed surreal. Claiming his mangled body had been all too real, though.

Only Teagan knew that Robert had moved out and that Elizabeth had talked to a divorce attorney. The kids thought he had been traveling for work, nothing unusual there. No one was more surprised than her when he'd volunteered to take her van and have one of his mechanic friends look at the brakes.

She'd thought the vehicle may need brake fluid, or a whole new set of brakes, and mentioned it to him the night before when he had called to explain why he hadn't put money in the household account for the mortgage payment. The next morning, she'd already caught a ride to work with a friend by the time he'd picked up her car. He was dead before she'd reached her desk.

Elizabeth released a heavy sigh as people continued to gather. She thought about everything she had yet to do that day, the next, and the one after that. She thought she was going to be okay financially...until yesterday. She scowled at the casket in front of her. Not only was the man inside a cheater, but he was also a thief.

She thought the house was covered by mortgage insurance. It was. Partially. Her knees had nearly given out when the bank officer informed her that Robert had taken out a second mortgage on the house...without her knowledge.

That house was hers. She'd bought it with a VA loan just as she was leaving the Army and going to work for the CIA. When she married Robert, she had his name added to the deed. The mortgage was paid out of their joint account. At least she'd been smart enough to insist they keep a separate bank account. Maybe, somewhere deep down, she never trusted him.

After mentally picking herself up off the floor, no one at the bank could adequately explain to her how Robert had gotten an equity loan without her knowledge. The new branch manager had carefully inferred that her predecessor and Robert had been extremely good friends. With his death, only the first mortgage had been paid off. Just one more thing she'd discovered about the deceiving bastard she'd married.

Emotionally she pounded another nail into the coffin in front of her.

As more people gathered around the tent, several moved onto what someday would be her grave site. When folks started standing four deep, Austin leaped out of his chair and raced to the other side.

"Move. Don't you dare stand on my father's grave." Her son started shoving people out of the way.

Within seconds, Micah was at Austin's side, taking charge and politely asking people to stand to the side. With his arm around her son's shoulder, they stood sentinel protecting Mason's grave.

Damn, she loved her team. Once again, they had her back.

Thankful tears filled her eyes and overflowed. Someone from the funeral home handed her another box of tissues. They had done an excellent job taking care of her and her family...and had helped immeasurably convincing Robert's parents of the need for the closed casket. He had run a busy red light and had been T-boned on the driver's side. Because of the severity of the accident, the insurance company had mandated an autopsy.

Elizabeth had been afraid her bad brakes had caused her husband's death. Thank God for her good friend, Gabriel. He'd come through for her once again. First on the mission when Mason died, and then he'd pulled some strings securing a copy of the medical examiner's report and the police accident report. Her brakes had been fine. Robert had been texting, more like sexting, when the accident happened. The Hispanic looking driver of the delivery truck that hit him had jumped out and ran away according to witnesses. It was really a shame that many of the street cameras in that area had been vandalized and were not functioning properly. The police considered it a hit and run and silently doubted they'd ever find the truck driver.

Replacing the old van was high on her to-do list after getting through the funeral. She could only keep the rental car another few days. Robert's car was a nearly new, two-seater convertible. How was she supposed to take both children to school in that? Thinking about cars made her glance toward the vehicles that lined the cemetery road.

She caught sight of a black sedan driving in and recognized it as Gabriel's official vehicle. He usually had a driver, but surprisingly her friend was behind the wheel, and someone she didn't recognize was in the passenger seat. Gabe had called her early that morning to let her know he wouldn't be able to make it to the church but would meet her at the cemetery. After parking, he got out, leaving the other man in the car. He briskly strode toward them but slowed when he answered his cell phone. His frown increased as he glanced back at his vehicle then toward the tent. Briefly, she wondered what had him so concerned. Had he discovered more information about Robert?

That was very self-centered thinking. Shame washed over her. He was the director of Special Activities Division that oversaw covert operations for the CIA. His paramilitary was always hunting the most dangerous men in the world. Of course the call wasn't anything dealing with her.

"Do you really think that crazy bitch will show up here?" Her mother leaned over and whispered in her ear.

Elizabeth's gaze found Logan who gave her the slightest head shake. He was on the lookout for Robert's latest squeeze, or anyone else who might try to make a scene like the one in the cathedral. Elizabeth couldn't help herself, she looked at his parents over her shoulder. They were holding up extremely well. They, too, had learned several things about their son that day.

She shuddered at the memory of the scene just an hour ago. As the priest started down the aisle, a woman Elizabeth didn't recognize tried to throw herself on the casket. Fortunately, Logan caught the blonde before she reached the end of the pew. When he tried to remove her from the church, she kicked and screamed, accusing Elizabeth of killing Robert because he was going to divorce Elizabeth to marry her. The woman was delusional.

The week before, Elizabeth had told Robert to get out, and had graciously given him ten minutes to pack what few clothes he kept at the house. He had begged her forgiveness, promising never to stray again, to be a better dad to his own daughter, and even try harder with Austin. Robert hadn't shown Liza much affection her entire life, claiming he didn't know what to do with babies or little girls. Her husband had given up years ago trying to be a father to her son. The kitchen and living room had become the demilitarized zone whenever he was home, since the children slept on the opposite end of the house from the master bedroom.

Elizabeth tried to remember the last time she and Robert had been intimate. Had he been fucking this other woman at the same time he'd been sleeping with her? Probably. All they had done in their bed for the past several months was sleep. She couldn't remember the last time they had made love. She was quite sure, though, that he had been inside the crazy blonde bitch very recently.

"No, Mom. I think the police finally came and took her away." At least that's what Logan had told her. She knew her husband's affair with the big boobed blonde wasn't his first, probably just the most current. The woman's breasts were enormous. Obviously enhanced—something Elizabeth had refused to do, no matter how much her husband begged for her to get them enlarged—she wondered if Robert had paid for the surgery. She didn't need anything that brought attention to her. That mindset may have been a carryover from her years in the Army, but it had kept her under the radar in the world of special operations. A good place to be when working for the CIA.

Movement in part of the cemetery caught her eye, but then she noticed it was just the man who came in the car with Gabe. He was striking with his nearly white hair and black moustache, his eyes hidden behind dark sunglasses. But it was his face that held her attention. The man was light years beyond handsome. She knew she was staring but she couldn't seem to take her eyes off him.

Her mother discreetly tapped her knee as the priest stepped to his position at the head of the casket. For the next twenty minutes Elizabeth dutifully focused her attention on the final part of the service. When instructed, she moved next to the priest to accept final condolences from those in attendance. She felt Gabriel move in directly behind her as Micah brought her son to the receiving line, then stood behind him. A quick glance over her shoulder confirmed that Teagan and Logan had joined them. Her former teammates had her back.

When the last guest was out of earshot, Elizabeth turned to her mother. "Mom, would you please walk the children back to the car?" She glanced toward Mason's grave. "We're going to take a few minutes."

Her mother smiled with understanding and took Liza by the hand. "Slide on those Jackie O sunglasses, sweetie." Bette Kamp instructed her granddaughter. "We need to protect our eyes," she explained as she slid on a matching pair of her own.

Damn, she loved her mother.

Elizabeth looked expectantly toward her son then dropped her gaze to the gravestone. He looked just like the picture of his father at that age, eyes like a lion, dark curly brown hair, and a firm jaw.

Micah, whose arm had never left the boy's shoulder

during the internment, gave him a nod. "Meet me at my truck. You can ride back to the house with me." He raised an eyebrow as he looked at her as though asking for approval.

Austin's face lit up, then his light brown eyes with a circle of gold surrounding the iris met hers. "Can I, Mom? Please?"

He was such a good kid, no matter what Robert had ever said about him. "Of course, you can." She tilted her head in the direction of her mother and Liza. "Go help your Gram—"

"I know, help Gram and Liza." He started to step away then turned and hugged the large SEAL. "Thanks, Uncle Micah. I'll be waiting for you with the truck."

Elizabeth didn't miss the slight twitch at the corners of her friend's mouth. Although he'd been married twice, Micah had never had children. She wondered if that was his choice. He'd make a great dad. He was only forty-three. It was still possible for him. The dad of one of Liza's playmates was pushing fifty. Sure, it was his second family and he had grown daughters, but he was the most loving father to that little girl. He'd made Robert look like an uncaring cad.

She glanced back at his grave. Robert had been an insensitive, self-centered ass. Liza didn't need a man like him as a role model for her future husband or the father of her children.

She stepped the six feet across the grass that would someday be her final resting place. Shaking her head, she couldn't believe the salesman had sold her so many plots. Inwardly she giggled. Maybe he knew something she didn't. She was only forty-one and had already buried two husbands. She was still young enough to marry at least once or twice more. But she'd be much more selective next time. Over the past week, she had all too often asked herself what she'd seen in Robert.

Her gaze fell upon Mason's headstone. She knew exactly why she'd fallen in love with him. He was the quiet type, introspective, intelligent, and very focused on whatever he was doing…especially if he was doing her. He'd been such an attentive lover, but he was also attuned to her needs out of bed as well as in it. That's what had gotten him killed, helping out the rest of the team because he could.

As they all surrounded Mason's grave, their emotional bond seemed to interlock. Teagan, Logan, Micah, and Gabriel had all been there when her world had blown up. She owed these people her life. They had kept her from running back into the still exploding building. She would have used her bare hands to dig through the debris to find Mason. But there was nothing left of him. The last time the five of them had stood there together, they had buried an empty casket. Just like he had done in Syria, Gabe had forced her to leave.

Her vision was blurred by tears when she looked at Gabriel. "I can't thank—" She couldn't finish the sentence. The man who arrived with Gabe now stood three feet behind him in the same spot her son had occupied for the past half hour. He'd taken off his reflective sunglasses and was wiping them with a lens cloth.

He looked up and met her gaze.

Elizabeth couldn't breathe. Her lungs refused to work.

She blinked, and blinked, trying to sweep away the water so she could focus. She removed her sunglasses and dabbed her eyes, then looked straight into his.

His whole body jolted as though they had been connected by a live wire.

No. It couldn't be.

Her gaze tracked to the gravestone. Mason A. Sinclair. She stared at the final date as if she needed confirmation of his death.

Slowly, she dared to look at the white-haired man with the face of an angel.

The edges of her vision narrowed until all she saw was his light brown eyes and the golden circle around the iris.

The world went black.

In her mind, she was falling into her own grave, meeting Mason in the next world, as every muscle in her body gave up.

CHAPTER SIX

Everyone in front of him scrambled, but Matt's feet were immovable.

The woman had fainted.

She'd looked straight at him, those stunning silvery eyes had rolled under her lids and she'd collapsed, neatly folding her lithe body into the fetal position.

It was those hypnotic eyes that held him in place. He'd recognize them anywhere. He'd seen them almost every night for months, years actually, in his dreams.

"Logan, call 911." The pretty blonde fell to her knees and tossed the woman's big black hat to the side before she gently rolled the limp body over.

Matt stared, leaning in, but staying put, out of the way, hoping to see those mesmerizing eyes once again.

"Delay that order, Logan. Let's not rush things," Gabe chided as he kneeled on the other side. "I think she just fainted. She's had a pretty rough day."

"You don't know the half of it, Gabe," the man with an unmistakable military bearing, obviously named Logan, shot back. "You missed the asshole's mistress accusing Elizabeth of murdering the cheating fucker."

Gabe's gaze flew to Logan's. "Christ, that's all she needed. She was already blaming herself for his death."

"Guys, we can discuss how this day was all kinds of fucked up, later." The blonde lifted the woman's knees to force blood to her friend's head. "We need to revive Elizabeth."

Elizabeth. She was Elizabeth. He instantly liked the name. It sounded right in his head. She looked like an Elizabeth. Her glossy hair seemed to sparkle in the bright sunshine. There were so many shades of brown, from light golden strands to nearly dark chocolate next to her neck.

"Micah, come around here and hold her head." The woman continued to give orders, and the men didn't argue.

Interesting.

"I don't think she hit it on anything, but you check it." She continued instructing everyone except him. Matt wasn't part of this cohesive team and that was fine with him. He was still stunned, unsure he could move.

The man in the navy-blue suit was already on the move. Something in the way he carried his body spoke of years of stealth training. Although his hair was longer than Logan's, he was either military or an agent, or both.

The woman and Gabe stretched Elizabeth out flat on her back, keeping her knees slightly bent before they rolled her torso and head to the side, in case she got sick while coming back to consciousness. "Logan, go see if the funeral home people have any cold water. We need a wet cloth."

"Sure thing, Teagan." Logan sprinted the few yards to where the funeral director was moving the massive flowers while others were taking down the tent.

So, the in-charge woman was Teagan. Matt liked that name, too. A helicopter flashed through his mind with her at the controls. How he knew it was her, he had no idea because between the helmet, face mask, and oxygen mask, it could have been anyone. But he was positive it was her.

He winced at the searing hot jab behind his left eye, and his hand automatically went there to massage his temple. The image was gone, and so was his pain.

"Elizabeth, time to wake up now." Teagan stroked her friend's forehead. The tenderness between the two women indicated they had been friends for a long time.

Gabe's familiarity with her was also obvious and as he unhesitatingly took her hand. "Elizabeth, we need you to come back to us now."

"No indication of head injury." Micah ceased running his fingertips through Elizabeth's hair. Matt didn't understand the jealousy that ran through him, but was extremely thankful that Elizabeth hadn't hit her head. He wondered if her hair was as soft as it looked. He imagined what it would feel like as he raked his fingertips over her scalp and straightened his fingers allowing the hairs to slip through and tickle the sensitive spot at the base of each digit.

Micah stared at the smattering of cars on the road. "Thank Christ her car is parked behind that big oak tree. Hopefully Austin and Liza can't see their mother lying on the ground."

Logan bounded toward them. "They had smelling salts." He handed the white capsule to Teagan.

Crushing the packet, Teagan immediately jerked back wincing. "I hate the smell of this fucking shit. They used it on us in flight school when we were in the oxygen deprivation chamber."

Micah's face scrunched as he turned it away. "Just wave it under her nose then get rid of it. Bad memories." Although, the big man didn't share.

Even Gabe looked away.

Elizabeth's eyes popped open as she tried to turn her head away. Her hands flew up as though to bat away the source of the smell.

"Stay down," Teagan ordered, spreading her free hand on Elizabeth's belly while flicking the capsule away like a discarded cigarette butt.

Micah moved his hands to her shoulders. "Just lie here a moment. We've got you." His voice was soft and filled with care.

"Wha…" Elizabeth's gaze darted from face to face. "What…" She shook her head as though to clear the fog. When she sucked in a deep breath, her face pinched and she laid her head back down. "What the hell happened?"

Teagan gave her a small smile. "You fainted."

Elizabeth rolled onto one elbow and slowly shook her head left to right. "I've never fainted in my life."

"Yes, you have." Logan smiled broadly. "One minute and forty-two seconds ago. You scared the shit out of us."

When Elizabeth tried to sit up, Teagan put a hand at her back and Micah helped lift her shoulders until she was upright. She looked straight at Teagan. "I really fainted?"

Her friend smiled and nodded. "Out cold."

As Elizabeth carefully looked at each of her friends, Matt's feet were finally able to move. He stepped back, intending to blend into the background, but he needed to stay close enough to see her crystalline eyes. They passed right over him as though he wasn't there. Disappointment washed through him.

"I'm fine, now." Elizabeth struggled slightly to get her feet underneath her. With the help of her friends, she rose gracefully then batted the grass clippings off her black, knee-length skirt.

"Let's get you home." Gabe placed his hand at the small of her back with a familiarity that deeply bothered Matt. He had no idea why his friend's actions troubled him so much. Gabe had told him that Elizabeth was a good friend. They had obviously known each other for quite a while. Matt wondered just how long, and how close their friendship actually was.

Before any one moved, as though in unison, they all looked at the headstone. Mason A. Sinclair. Captain, U.S. Special Forces. The dates of his birth and death.

Matt memorized every word. Out of his peripheral vision, a white folded paper skipped across the grave behind him. With everyone else's attention on Elizabeth and the final resting place of their friend, in two steps he snagged the paper. After a quick glance, he quietly folded the program from the cathedral and stuffed it in his pants pocket. All the information he needed to start a search was now at his fingertips.

He'd find out more about her. He had to. For some reason, she was extremely important to him. If his dreams were truly visions of the future, she would become one of the most important things in his life.

As the five friends started back toward the cars, Gabe looked at Matt as though seeing him for the first time. He hand-signaled using a special language all CIA Special Operators learn: *Is there a problem?*

Matt quickly replied in the same secret language: *No. Muscles were cramping. Needed to walk. Is the woman okay? Need help?*

Gabe: *Thanks. We've got this.*

Matt noticed the other two men watching their fingers and hand gestures with a look of confusion. This was exactly the reason the Special Activities Division had developed their own language for the Special Operations Group. Although almost all SAD Operators were former SEALs, Army Special Forces, or Marine SpecOps, their SOG brotherhood was much like the CIA itself, beyond secretive, exclusive and silent.

Gabe glanced at Elizabeth's friends then to Matt. Several steps later, he signaled for Matt to join them. Intersecting them from the side, Gabe slowed to a stop. He turned slightly to face Elizabeth and as if checking to be sure she was all right. His gaze then passed over the rest as they formed a semicircle. "Everyone, I would like you to meet Matthew St. Clare. He's my next in command as deputy director of Special Activities Division." With a sheepish smile, he added, "We have an appointment in an hour at the Pentagon. I'm sorry, Elizabeth, but I won't be able to stop by the house until later this evening."

"That's okay, Gabe." She looked to the others in the group then managed a small smile. "The team will keep me busy."

Matt didn't miss the word team. Had these five worked together…as a team? When? Where? And how? In his world, team meant covert operators inside a dangerous situation. He slid a glance back toward the army captain's grave. Had Mason A. Sinclair been on that same team?

"Matt, I'd like to introduce you to Elizabeth Kamp, Teagan Williams, Logan Jackson, and Micah Reid." Gabe had been staring intently at him, watching as though he was testing Matt's social skills.

When he took Elizabeth's small soft hand in his, he lightly squeezed it so as not to hurt her. Although she didn't seem like a delicate bloom, he'd always been aware of his own strength. What he hadn't expected was the warmth that emanated from her fingers to run up his arm and seemed to touch his soul, reaffirming that he still had one. After everything he'd done in his life, it came as a surprise.

"Nice to meet you. I'm sorry it wasn't under better circumstances. I'm sorry for your loss." Matt was pleased indeed that he could string together three coherent sentences. If he had looked into her eyes, he couldn't have uttered a single syllable. Thankfully those beautiful blue-grays were hidden behind dark sunglasses that stretched above her eyebrows and over part of her cheekbones.

"I'm sorry I interrupted your work day." She tried a smile but failed as she released his hand. "I'm sure you and Gabe need to get back on the road. It's nearly a forty-five-minute drive in good traffic to the Pentagon." She looked over at Logan and Micah and gave them a genuine smile. "The military brass doesn't like it when us agency types keep them waiting."

If that wasn't a dismissal, Matt had never heard one. Hurrying, he took Teagan's hand. "Pleasure to meet you." After a single small shake, he released her strong fingers and stepped in front of Logan. Taking the man's hand, he commented, "Are you still in the military?"

Logan squeezed his hand and nodded. "MARSOC commanding officer." He tilted his head toward Gabe. "He's been trying to recruit me for ten years. I'm not yet ready to retire but when I do, I'm out of the game."

"I understand." Matt moved on, extending his hand to Micah. "Ditto, except I'm commanding officer Naval Special Warfare Group 2." He shook his head. "Not interested in a new job."

"Good to know." In truth, Matt had no desire to recruit anyone into SOG. That wasn't his job, nor was Gabe's, which made their responses even more interesting. As if given a hidden cue, everyone started walking again.

As they trekked in silence, Matt found it fascinating that all three of the other men were in charge of about one thousand highly trained, lethal soldiers, sailors, and Marines. All were involved in special operations. All were the best of the best. Then there was Elizabeth and Teagan who seemed right at home in the mix.

When they reached a paved road, Matt reluctantly peeled off and waited next to the company sedan. He wanted so badly to again see those gorgeous silver eyes with a hint of blue, the color of Alaskan glaciers. The thick paper in his pocket crinkled as he walked so he moved it to the inside chest pocket of his suit jacket. He didn't want Gabe asking any questions.

As his boss approached the car, Matt slid into the passenger seat. On the slow drive out of the cemetery, Gabe warned, "Just because I introduced you to Elizabeth, doesn't mean you can call her and ask her out. She's a grieving widow."

Matt slowly turned his head to look at Gabe. "What kind of fucking asshole do you think I am?"

"You're the asshole who can see even the slightest opportunity and take advantage of it." Gabe took his eyes off the road, glancing at him. "Exactly what I've trained you to be, completely mission oriented." Returning his gaze to the one-way, narrow blacktop, he added, "Elizabeth is not your personal mission. There are plenty of other women out there for you to fuck, then fuck over. She's a lifetime commitment." The corner of his mouth twitched. "Sometimes that lifetime only lasts five years."

Matt studied his boss of the corner of his eye. Had Gabe killed Elizabeth's husband? Or had him killed? They were now both single. Matt didn't like the idea of Gabe with Elizabeth, now that he'd met her. She was supposed to be his future...if his dreams, or visions, or whatever the fuck they were, became real

~

Six hours later, Matt checked in on the Operations Center, dropping his car keys and laptop on the command desk.

Justin paced, watching the wall of screens, as he calmly spoke into the headset ordering the U.S. Navy to be ready to send helicopters into an African nation to extract a SOG team. His men were very close to crossing someone off the Most Wanted List.

"How did the Pentagon briefing go?" Justin tapped the microphone off as he sat on the edge of the desk.

"Same shit, different day." Matt pointed to the list in the upper right of the gigantic screen. "USSOCOM wants to fuck with the list. They want us to play nice with their boys...and girls."

"No shit." Justin stood and scanned the immediate area. Just above a whisper, he asked, "Did the new general confirm that they have an all-female team?"

Matt grinned. "He didn't deny it. And he used the term, my men and women more than once. You could've heard a pin drop in the silence that followed those words."

"Holy fuck." Justin quickly scanned the wall of live feed then returned his attention to Matt as he parked his butt against the semi-circular command desk. "You know there's a rumor that Tom Gillpatrick's niece, Katlin Calahan, is one of them. They supposedly work for that jerkoff Jack Ashford over in Homeland Security. I've been told, by a reliable source, that they're call the Black Swans."

Matt was too was curious to let that one go. "Black Swans? That's a weird name. Why aren't they called the Birds of Prey? Or the Talons Team? Something more dangerous sounding?"

"Fuck if I know." Justin scanned the huge wall of moving pictures. He shrugged returning his attention to Matt. "Maybe it has something to do with that guy's theory of financial Black Swan events changing the world."

Matt smiled. "Yeah. Women in SpecOps would change the world. Can you imagine the gossip mill then? And if the media got even a whiff of that story? This place is rampant with rumors. For an intelligence agency, we sure are a gossipy bunch."

Justin laughed. "Good thing we only gossip about each other." He glanced around the room. "No one here would dare to speak of the things they hear and see in this building."

"They value their life too much." The internal rumor mill was one of the things Matt wanted to tap into. But he had other needs first. He lifted his computer. "I'm having a few problems with my unit. Do you have the geek doing anything important?"

They both looked toward the glassed-in area where a boy was tearing a computer apart, had three others in pieces and simultaneously watched five screens. "He's not busy tonight. We have a few units down, but they've been replaced."

Red lights started blinking, and both men looked up at the wall.

"Need help?" Matt offered.

"I got this." Justin tapped his mic. "Sit rep."

Matt walked into what they fondly referred to as the Geek Cave. A computer expert was on duty twenty-four-seven. SAD couldn't afford a computer failure in the middle of a mission. Lives were always at stake.

He looked at the name badge and felt terribly sorry for the young man. He must have been beat up in school every day. He's probably now making ten times what those bullies bring home. "Clarence, I have—"

The kid never looked up. "Just set it on the stack to the right of the door. Unless I'm told different from the boss man, they're taken in order."

Matt withheld a chuckle. "Well, since I am the boss man, you will—"

"Oh." The boy looked up. "Shit." He stood, and the

computer he'd been working on fell to the floor, but he kept his gaze on Matt. "Mr. St. Clare." He glanced at the very broken computer screen on the floor. "Sir." He started to kneel to retrieve the parts scattered across the tile but changed his mind and stood at attention.

The kid was so flustered Matt decided to cut him a break. "You can talk to me as you pick up all those pieces."

"Thank you, Mr. St. Clare." He kneeled and started collecting parts. Then he looked up in confusion. "How can I help you?"

This is where things got a bit tricky. Matt knew the space was not bugged and there were no cameras pointed in that direction, but what he wanted wasn't exactly sanctioned. He wasn't even sure he had the authority to ask the geek to do this.

"I want to understand why we can't catch some of these men when they use a computer every day to conduct illegal business." Matt pointed his thumb toward the operations center. "How do they do it?"

Clarence stared at him from his position on the floor. "You want me to tell you how they avoid our traces?"

"Yes. Exactly." This was going to be easier than Matt had thought.

"Sir, I'm not allowed to do that." He twisted his acne-scarred face as though in thought. Then he rapid-fired questions. "Is this a test? Did someone question my loyalty to the CIA? To the United States? They said in my training classes that we might be tested."

Thinking quickly, Matt explained, "No. This is not a test." He purposely looked embarrassed and glanced at the huge sloping room. "Look, Clarence, I don't want any of the others to know how non-tech I am. I can run SOG teams all over the world, but I can't understand why we can't track everything they do on their computers. What are they doing to make their computers untraceable? I need to understand how they do it. How far can they go with it?"

Clarence picked up several parts. "You want me to explain to you how ghosting software works?"

"Is that what they use so we can't track what they're looking at online?" Now he was getting somewhere. He'd have to buy ghosting software.

The young man stood with a handfuls of parts. "That's part of it. They also have throw-away computers." He set the pieces on his workbench. "And it's not like you buy a ghosting program from the ap store."

Fuck. Matt was going to need more than a little help just to do some off-the-books research. "I learn different from you younger men. I need to learn through hands-on. That's the way I gain a deeper understanding, by doing it myself."

Clarence gave him a pitying look. "I get it. My grandfather has no idea what I do and when I try to explain it to him, he thinks I can fix his TV. He's about your age, I guess." Then he quickly added, "but he's retired. He might be a bit older than you."

Matt had never felt so old in his life.

"I obviously need your help, a lot. But this needs to be our secret." Matt jerked his thumb toward the command center.

The boy's eyes lit up. "Yes, sir. I understand. Will we have a code word? Do you need me to buy you a throw away computer? We have some really outstanding programs we use here that I can get loaded for you. One of my friends is upstairs in cyber security, and she lets me test her newest code to see if I can get around it."

"Is that where you'd like to work?" Matt suggested.

"Oh, yes, sir." Then he quickly said, "But this job requires a really high security clearance too. There's lots of people who want my job. I like it here. No one bothers me unless their unit crashes and we have loaners, so I can take my time fixing everything right." As though a lightbulb went off, Clarence dug around the small space and handed Matt a computer. "Use this one for a while. You can search anything on the Net and no one here can trace it."

"Really?" This was too good to be true. "What if I need to use some of the search programs I have on my computer?"

"No problem. I've loaded it with everything our SOG teams use in the field." It was his turn to look sheepish. "It's a prototype I was building for our guys. It has a titanium case that's shielded to withstand an EMP. That's an—"

"I know all about electromagnetic pulses. I've even used them. Go on." This kid was brilliant. He was thinking ahead and working to meet the needs of the future, not just repairing hardware and software problems.

"This program we're working on, with my friend upstairs, will help keep the bad guys from tracking our teams." Clarence shoved the computer at him. "You can test it for us." A second later, he added, "Sir."

"Thank you, Clarence. I'll let you know what I think." As Matt was about to leave, he turned back to the young man. "Good work."

CHAPTER SEVEN

Three Days Later

It was only ten thirty in the morning, and it had already been one hell of a day. Elizabeth wondered if it was too early to have a glass of wine. Nix that idea. She needed a shot of smooth Scotch.

She opened the refrigerator and sighed heavily. She really needed to do some grocery shopping. Grabbing the remains of the cranberry juice and one of Liza's apple flavored juice boxes, she poured them into the last clean glass in the cupboard. Thank God the dishwasher was almost finished. She'd forgotten to hit the button to start the load before falling into bed last night.

Apple cranberry is a real drink. Right? It is now. Tentatively she sipped. *Not bad.* It would be even better with rum. Vodka would be okay, too. Nobody could smell that on her breath. Too bad there wasn't any in the house.

Robert's family had eaten everything in her refrigerator

and pantry after devouring all the casseroles the ladies of the church had delivered. His brothers had hit the well-stocked bar before Elizabeth had even returned from the cemetery. Without invitation, his three brothers and their wives, seven elementary school age children between them, had decided to camp out in her basement family room and use her house as a base for sightseeing in Washington, D.C. for the weekend *since they were already there,* and *the children may never have this opportunity again.*

Like Elizabeth didn't already have enough stress.

Thankfully, they had all left Sunday after she made four dozen pancakes, fried three pounds of bacon, and scrambled thirty-four eggs with cheese. Then she made a special egg-white omelet for the bitchy wife of brother number two who insisted on using her shower in the master bedroom rather than the guest shower in the basement or the one her children shared.

Elizabeth had never been so grateful to see people leave. She was even more relieved that she would never have to see those rude people again in her life.

Then she entered the basement and her initial relief vanished, replaced by anger and resolve.

Even with the help of her children, it had taken three hours to clean up the mess. Austin hauled five garbage bags up the stairs and out to the trash cans. Liza's little legs made fourteen trips up to the laundry room. Elizabeth scrubbed the bathroom for more than an hour before she was satisfied it was clean. She'd have to call a carpet cleaning service to remove the stains. She didn't have the energy to do it herself. By Sunday night, she was so exhausted they had pizza delivered.

As she had crawled into bed that night, so tired she could barely move, she thanked God that the worst was over.

Monday morning proved her wrong. Liza had a meltdown, the kind only a four-year-old can throw, over the lack of her favorite cereal. Austin wanted to take the entire week off school...to celebrate. She finally wrangled both children to the car and got them to school and had even remembered notes for their days absent. Her next stop was the bank.

It took more than an hour for the branch manager to find five minutes to speak to her, only to be told that she needed an official death certificate—with a raised seal—and an official copy of their marriage license before they could open Robert's personal safe deposit box and close his personal checking account. Since she'd never changed her last name, keeping her maiden name, she had to prove they'd been married. That was understandable. Elizabeth knew exactly where their marriage certificate was located, in her safe deposit box in a completely different bank.

She'd vowed while sitting there, people watching, that she would take every dime out of that bank and never recommend them to anyone, even those people she didn't like. Her attitude toward the bank didn't change when she stood to leave and the manager, frowning at the computer screen, and asked her to sit back down. Closing Robert's account wasn't going to be difficult at all. They would simply apply those funds to the credit card, leaving her only $6,852.37 to pay.

"But my name isn't even on that credit card," she insisted.

"Virginia is a joint property state." The pompous ass leaned his forearms on the desk and smiled as he announced, "If you write me a check for that amount right now, there won't be any additional interest added to the amount owed."

Elizabeth was an intelligent woman and saw this as a bartering opportunity. Coyly, she pulled her checkbook out of her purse. "So, you recognize me as Robert's wife by asking me to pay off his credit card, is that right?"

"Oh, yes. You showed me a *copy* of his death certificate, and your driver's license. That's all we need to cash the check." His grin was smug, especially when he added, "We will need for your check to clear, and that might take a few days, before we can completely close out all of his accounts here. Don't worry about the interest accumulated during that time, I'll see to it that the bank covers it."

He wanted her to be thankful that the bank was going to cover a few pennies of interest while they waited for her money? Oh, no. She would never give him that satisfaction. She plucked a pen with the bank logo on it from a cup sitting on her side of the desk. "So, as soon as I hand you this check, we can walk into the vault and we can open the safe deposit box."

The rotund man sat up so fast he almost fell out of the chair. "No. No. We need the official death certificate, with the raised seal, and your marriage license, also with the raised seal." He straightened his tie. "We have procedures we must follow."

She snapped the checkbook closed and stood. "Since you're not willing to let me into that safe deposit box, which by law is now mine, I don't see the need to pay off Robert's debts, which I had nothing to do with. Hell, I didn't even know about that credit card." She turned to leave but only made it one step.

"When can we expect your check?" He pressed. "This has to be paid or we'll have no choice but to sue the estate."

She slowly turned. "Maybe you should ask the blonde with fake boobs he was fucking to pay the money back. He never spent a dime of it on me or his children."

Fuming and frustrated, she'd stormed out of the bank.

Elizabeth let out a long, heavy sigh. Sipping the

concoction, she knew she'd have to take that pompous ass the documents in order to find what little treasures Robert had stashed in his safe deposit box. Maybe it was cash. Gold bars would be nice. But they'd be too heavy for a box like that. Diamonds. They are light weight and small. With her luck, it would be some kind of stupid shit like his participation award for sixth grade soccer.

She didn't have time to think about that anymore.

Before she picked up the kids, she'd swing by her bank and get out their marriage license. She'd probably need it for other things as well since their last names were different. She was now very happy with her decision five years ago to keep her maiden name. She didn't have to change her driver's license or her Social Security or passport. Yeah, it could prove problematic while closing out everything that belonged to Robert, but she wouldn't have his last name as a constant reminder. Maybe she'd even change Liza's last name to Kamp.

She stared around the silent kitchen. Except the fact that she was home in the middle of the day, not much had changed. She needed to get back to work. They had given her a week to settle everything, but she was ready to return to their normal everyday life without Robert. The only difference would be that he was never coming home again. It wouldn't be the first time she'd moved on after burying a husband, although this time was very different.

Her heart still ached every time she thought about Mason, but she had reached the final stage of acceptance just before she left the Army. She was deep in the second stage of anger with Robert. There wouldn't be any stage III bargaining and Elizabeth was pretty sure she would skip the stage four depression and slide straight into acceptance.

She got up to empty and reload the dishwasher, still

catching up from her in-laws visit, when the front doorbell rang.

Glancing at the side table next to the door, she debated on grabbing her gun then shunned the idea. She peered through the peep hole. The man with white hair looked familiar, but she'd met so many men in the last week, she couldn't place him. Was he from Robert's office? Or a bill collector? He wore a nice suit over wide shoulders and was that a shoulder holster? Yes. Was he a plain clothes cop? Or had the agency sent him?

Only one way to tell. She opened the door as far as the chain would allow. "Can I help you?"

"I hope you can." He handed his identification through the crack in the door. "I'm Matthew St. Clare. We met at the cemetery a few days ago. I'm sorry for your loss."

Okay, he looked like the man in the picture, and the leather covered ID said he was CIA. She moved the case to see the iridescent hologram of the agency's seal. Supposedly, that feature couldn't be copied which meant it was probably real.

"What can I do for you Senior Special Agent St. Clare?" She handed him back the wallet-like ID holder.

She stared at him, but couldn't see his eyes behind the sunglasses.

"May I come in? This may take a while." His words surprised her. What could he have to say that could take much time?

She made a show of checking her watch. "I can give you a few minutes." She closed the door enough to release the chain, then held it open. "Please come in." She showed him to the living room where she sat in a wingback chair and offered him the other one several feet away. Popping up she apologized, "Excuse my manners. Would you like something to drink?" Then she considered her empty refrigerator. "I can offer you a glass of cold water."

"No, thank you, I'm fine." He'd stood when she rose and waited in front of the designated chair until she sat down.

Manners. That's a nice surprise. "Now, what's this all about?" His presence in her living room wasn't though. What the hell did the agency want now?

He took off his sunglasses and slid them into the breast pocket of his gray suit jacket. His gaze swept the room as he took in everything. It had been a long time since she'd been in the company of a man like him. He was like Mason had been. Always cataloging his surroundings, aware of every exit and potential danger. He looked everywhere but at her.

Then, as though the last puzzle piece clicked into place, his eyes met hers. "Your husband's recent death has initiated an investigation into the death of Mason Sinclair."

All the air left her lungs.

She wasn't sure if it was what he'd said or the way he stared at her, almost accusingly. That wasn't anywhere close to what she had expected him to say, and she'd thought she was prepared for anything. Elizabeth slumped back into the soft cushions. "What do the two deaths, ten years apart, have to do with each other?"

"Probably nothing, but you are a common denominator and you have a high security classification." He leaned forward and put his forearms on his thighs. "We have some questions about what happened when your first husband was killed."

"Did you already talk to Gabriel Davis?" Why hadn't Gabe filled in any blanks they may have. He had been there, running the op on the ground. She studied the man for a second. He'd arrived at the cemetery with Gabe. "Don't you work for him? Did he send you here?"

His posture turned defensive. "No, ma'am. Matter of fact,

we prefer that you don't mention any of this inquiry to Director Davis." Then he quickly added, "Or anyone else. This is an internal investigation."

Was Gabe in trouble? As his friend, she should warn him. On the other hand, she knew how to keep a secret. Was this a test in her vetting process? Had they found out about Robert's debt? She still didn't know where all the money had gone. At least she had her own, separate accounts. High debt was a key trigger for a new round of vetting. If she wasn't careful, she could lose her job. She wouldn't want Gabe to know her personal business either way.

"Elizabeth."

The sound of her name brought her out of her thoughts. "I'm sorry. What did you say?"

"Can you keep this conversation, and any subsequent conversations we may have, completely confidential and this investigation a secret?" Those brown and gold eyes pierced her, as though he could see all the way to her soul. It was a good thing she was already sitting down. It was as though an invisible force had punched her in the sternum. Secrets. Mason's death. Don't tell. It was as though his gaze had shoved those words at her.

This was a deeper vetting. She'd hit the nail on the head. Besides, most of that failed mission was already in the books. She wasn't sure if she could add anything after all these years. Maybe he was going to cross check anything she told him against what the files showed, checking her memory. She'd already screwed up by losing track of the conversation.

"Of course, I can and will." She tried to put as much confidence in her voice as possible.

He seemed pleased by her answer as he held her gaze. His eyes. There was something about those beautiful brown eyes. They were so much like her son's. Coincidence. That was all it was. The shape of his eyes was different. His were rounder and harder than Austin's almond like, soft understanding eyes that went with his old-soul personality.

"I've read the reports, but I'd like you to walk me through the mission." He gave her a small, encouraging smile that she appreciated.

No! That meant she'd have to relive that day, open that wound again, right after she'd buried her second husband. Not that dealing with Robert's death hurt anywhere near what it should. Just knowing she'd have to talk about Mason tightened her throat.

"Are you familiar with the part of the mission that was a test project placing active duty men and women together in a combat situation?" She wondered how much he really knew.

"I'm aware of the initial parameters of the personnel and the project." He shifted in his seat then asked, "You and Captain Sinclair were involved in an intimate relationship. Do you believe if those overseeing the test program knew that fact they would eliminate one or both of you from the mission?"

Elizabeth knew the answer, but it showed a character flaw. "No one needed to know about our relationship. That was private. By the time we arrived for that mission, we were married so it was more than just an intimate relationship."

"You evaded the question." He cocked his head to the side very slightly. A flash of familiarity screamed through her brain. Someone she knew used to do that when she wouldn't answer his question. The thought was gone as quickly as it appeared.

"No, I corrected your premise." She'd answer the damn question. "Of course, they would have pulled us from the mission and kicked us out of the program." She quickly added, "But Mason knew how important it was to me. We worked side by side visiting villages throughout Iraq for nearly eight months. We had a coed team, and we accomplished our goals and missions. And, yes, Mason and I fell in love in the dusty desert, sleeping in smelly tents and eating meals prepared from a bag. There were other women on the team and no one else left as a couple. I wanted the brass to know that men and women could work side by side, under fire, and be a solid unit."

"So, you and Captain Sinclair knew each other before you were selected for the joint task force?" He gave her that reassuring smile once again. "How did you meet?"

"Mason." She choked on his name. It took her a few seconds before she could tamp down the emotions that were always present with thoughts of him. "Mason and I had known each other at West Point but hadn't dated there. We were just friends. When we were stationed together at Fort Campbell in Kentucky, he was with the 5th Special Forces Group – Alpha, and I was with their Intelligence support. We spent a lot of time together. We'd dated for over a year before we'd both been sent to Iraq. I'm not sure whose idea it was for the female linguists to go into the camps and villages to gather human intelligence from the women, but it was brilliant. Training and intelligence are also missions of the Green Berets. Combining our efforts was a stroke of genius."

All he did was nod. Matthew St. Clare was a quiet one. Hard to read too, but as he rubbed his temple, she could see he was hurting.

"I have some heavy-duty ibuprofen if you'd like some," she offered. She stood and like a gentleman, so did he.

Though he hesitated at first, he capitulated. "That would be wonderful."

"You wait right there, and I'll get it for you." She dashed to her bathroom and grabbed the bottle, prescription strength medicine she took for her monthly cramping. The older she got, the more she looked forward to menopause and being done with periods forever. She didn't want any more children, not that it was even a possibility now. She'd never allow herself to fall in love again. She couldn't put herself and her children through that pain once more.

Bottle in hand, she passed through the living room to the kitchen. Grabbing a glass from the dishwasher, she stuck it under the ice dispenser on the fridge door. "Agent St. Clare," she called, her attention on the ice dropping into the glass.

"Yes, Elizabeth?" His voice was deep and right behind her.

She flinched.

"I'm so sorry, I didn't mean to frighten you." He looked at her sheepishly. "I was just eager for the medicine."

He wasn't exactly crowding her, but he was close. She was surprised she didn't feel defensive. There was something about him that made her feel extremely comfortable in his presence, even though he was within her personal space.

She handed him the glass then shook out one pill onto her palm. "These are eight hundred milligrams, that's the equivalent of four over the counter pills. You can only take four of these a day."

He gently touched her bicep. Heat immediately radiated from that point and swept throughout her body. She looked into his eyes now filled with concern. "Elizabeth, are you sick?"

Embarrassed, she glanced away. "No." Her grandmother's phrase popped into her head. "For situations only a woman can understand." Let him guess what that means. She had practically lived on Vitamin I, as she and her girlfriends had called it, during training for both the Army and the CIA. In the desert, the huge white pills were handed out like candy to whiny children. There was nothing better for sore muscles and joints than ibuprofen.

He popped the pill then washed it down with the entire

glass of water. "May I?" He nodded toward the refrigerator dispenser.

"Certainly." She reached to take the glass and their hands brushed. Soft tingles ran up her arm, and she jerked her hand away.

His pupils dilated, but he controlled his body better than she did hers.

"I've got this." He stepped closer and shoved the glass against the bar. The sound of water pouring over ice filled the silence in the kitchen. "Mind if I take this back with me to the living room?" He grinned. "I promise to use a coaster."

Elizabeth's knees almost gave out. The use of coasters had been an ongoing battle with all the men in her life. First with Mason, who would often set a sweating glass down on a wood surface then forget about it, then with Austin. She'd find his leaking juice boxes everywhere when he was a child and when he was promoted to sippie cups, they'd leave rings on all her good furniture. At nine years old, she'd considered him trained, at least well enough to use coasters. When she and Robert had first started dating, the man never thought about water rings, but he had learned fast when she started pointing to the stack of coasters before he even had an opportunity to set a drink down.

A mental snapshot of her family room furniture flashed through her mind. All her ruined coffee tables and end tables were down there, now bearing even more damage circles from wet spots thanks to her in-laws. Someday, she'd replace it with nicer furniture after it survived the high school years and the basement filled with teens.

"Some woman has taught you well." She gave him a genuine smile.

"My first serious girlfr..." He winced in pain as his hand shot up to his temple, and he massaged the area over his white sideburns.

She marveled at his beautiful smooth skin. His age was hard to guess. He had very few wrinkles, neither laugh lines bracketing his mouth nor the small fan of lines at the corner of his eyes that deepened as men aged from either squinting or smiling. Perhaps he was one of those men genetically disposed to gray early. He was more than handsome, he was beautiful. If it weren't for the hard edge that oozed from every pore in his body, he'd be downright pretty. At least now she knew he was straight. Why that made any difference, she had no idea, but somewhere deep it was reassuring.

Her gaze dropped to the nearly black moustache that rode over his top lip. She'd never kissed a man with a moustache and wondered what it would be like. Was it stiff and scratchy or soft? Would it tickle as he kissed her lips? Her breasts? Her— She had no business wondering about her inquisitor, least of all days after burying her husband, even if he had been a self-centered lover and cheating bastard. It had been months since she'd had sex, neither had been interested. Perhaps she simply longed for the gentle touch of a man.

Her mouth went dry as her gaze scanned his very fit body. "Before we continue, I think I'll grab a glass of water, also. Please take a seat, I'll be right there." Elizabeth took a few minutes to mentally regroup. Returning to the living room, she found him standing in front of the fireplace, not just looking, but seeming to absorb every picture on the mantle. He was holding Austin's most recent school picture.

He slid her a glance as she approached. "Handsome young boy. How old is he?"

"He just turned nine." She smiled with pride and as she stepped closer and looked at the boy who would all too soon be a man. "They grow up so fast."

Without looking at her, he asked, "Is he Mason Sinclair's son?"

She didn't bother to look at the agent. "Yes." She

swallowed a sip of water, hoping to wash down the lump that had formed in her throat. "Austin looks more like his father every day." She didn't want to discuss her children with this man. She lifted the picture from his hands and returned it to the mantle. "I need to go pick up the children soon. Are we almost finished?"

"No." He drank the rest of the water and strode to the kitchen where he set the glass in the sink. She'd followed him. "You have things to do. Why don't we plan on meeting later in the week? When do you expect a return to work?"

"I still have several loose ends to tie up tomorrow, so probably Wednesday." At least she hoped she could get everything completed by then.

"When is the best time for you to meet, privately?" He glanced around the house. "Your children need you right now, and I don't want to take away your time from them."

Damn. This man was being so accommodating. Usually in the vetting process, they set the time and place and you were expected to show up, changing any plans you had for that time frame. She had to think a minute. "I have to go over to headquarters on Thursday. Perhaps we can meet when I'm finished with my briefing. We could find an empty conference room."

"No. I'd rather not meet there," he quickly responded. "If anyone sees us together, they may start asking questions. At this point in the investigation, neither of us want that."

She had to agree with his reasoning. "How about Thursday morning, before I go to Langley? Can we meet here? I'd normally go into the office first, but I can just head straight to headquarters when we're finished."

He looked so pleased at her compromise. "That will work perfectly for me as well."

She followed him to the door where he took her hand and shook it lightly. "I'll see you right here on Thursday morning." He gave her hand a slight squeeze. Until then, she hadn't realized he was still holding it.

When he slid his hand from hers and opened the door, she suddenly missed the warmth he'd brought to her whole body.

By the way she was looking forward to seeing Matthew St. Clare again, Thursday almost felt like a date.

CHAPTER EIGHT

Three Days Later

As Matthew rang the bell to Elizabeth's home, he felt so much more prepared than he had on Monday. He had been extremely nervous, totally unsure of his reception but by the time he left, he felt as though he had made a real connection with the very pretty brunette. This time she opened the door completely, without hesitation.

"Good morning, Agent St. Clare." Her greeting included a smile that made it all the way to her eyes.

"Elizabeth." He held out his hand. When she gave him hers, he simply held it. "Thank you so much for agreeing to meet with me again today." Dressed similarly to the first time he'd seen her at headquarters, she looked professional. Her eyes were no longer red and puffy. She seemed very sharp compared to a few days ago.

"How's your head?" Her casual question took him aback for a second.

In truth, the headaches were coming more and more

often, attacking him at the strangest times. But he had spent long hours in small coffee shops and local libraries, skipping off their Wi-Fi networks as he conducted his covert research into her background and the incident in Syria ten years ago.

Matt decided to tell her the truth. "They come and go. Sometimes it's worse than others."

They returned to the same seats in the living room. He knew her time was limited, as was his. "If you don't mind, let's get started. When we left off, I believe you were telling me what happened when you and Captain Sinclair returned from your tour together in Iraq."

Elizabeth took a deep breath and let it out slowly as though she was fortifying herself. "As soon as we got back to the United States, we were reassigned to the Joint Special Operations Command at Fort Bragg, North Carolina. We met the rest of our new team and trained together for weeks before we were assigned that mission to Syria. You met Teagan, Logan, and Micah at...the other day." She forced a smile. "We all became very tight, extremely fast. In the field as well as out."

The first part of that information coincided with what he'd read in the files. Their strong personal connection wasn't news because he'd seen that for himself, although official files only noted their cooperative attitude during working hours. What he hadn't found, though, was the marriage certificate. Interrupting, he asked, "And you were married then?"

"No, Mason and I got married the night before we left North Carolina for Syria. No one knew." She emphasized the last sentence as though she needed to make that point perfectly clear. "Our team had become good friends, but Mason and I hadn't had the opportunity to tell them. Even our parents didn't know until..." She swallowed hard. "After the explosion..." She rolled her lips in as though to keep them from quivering. He watched her fight to leash her emotions. "There was a SEAL team close by. They went in to try to recover…" She looked away. Her breathing was ragged as she visibly struggled with the memories. It took her a few minutes before she returned her gaze to him. "There was nothing left."

Matt couldn't stand to see her in such pain. He moved over and sat at the end of the couch, the closest seat to her. He took her hand in his. Somehow, it felt right. "Elizabeth, I know this is difficult, but I need to know everything that happened leading up to the explosion."

She nodded. "Our mission was to destroy a munitions cache, supposedly provided by the Russians to Nassar al Jamil."

At the mention of the familiar terrorist, Matt's head started to hurt, but he refused to let go of her hand. He wanted to comfort this woman, take away her agony. A protectiveness he didn't know existed within him had roared to the surface. He would endure this damn headache, hiding his own pain, in order to ease hers. He was the reason she was suffering. Well aware of his own deception, part of him hated putting her through this inquisition, but he needed to find answers. She had haunted him for years and he wasn't about to stop questioning her now.

"It was Mason's job to take the terrorist out if given the opportunity, but at the last-minute intel said al Jamil was forty miles away being chased by a SEAL team." Elizabeth sniffed and grabbed a tissue from the box on the corner table. Matt released her hand and immediately regretted the loss of connection. "Mason had helped place the charges. One went off early, triggering all them to detonate before he got out." She burst into tears.

Matt stood and pulled her into his arms, holding her as she sobbed. He usually hated being around crying women, but Elizabeth was bringing out a side of him he'd never seen before. He wanted to comfort her. Holding her felt...right. Almost familiar. His head pounded but instead of rubbing his temples, he gently moved his hand up and down her spine.

"He wasn't even supposed"—Sniff. Gasp.—"to be inside the building." Her entire body shook, rapt with sorrow.

Matt didn't know whether to feel like an ass for forcing her to recount what had to be one of the most terrible days of her life or be thankful that he was getting to the truth. Holding her in his arms was certainly no hardship. As he inhaled, the scent of citrus and spice filled his senses. She smelled clean and fresh. He wanted to bury his face in her soft hair, bathe in her goodness, and wash away all the evil in the world he faced every day in that dark room where he sat in the command center.

And Nassar al Jamil seemed to be woven through the fabric of his life. Yesterday, he'd watched four of his best men die at the hands of the terrorist's men. They weren't even after him! The gun dealer they were pursuing turned out to be one of al Jamil's suppliers and they caught him midst a transaction. Matt closed his mind to that scene and used the woman in his arms to erase the image. His pain was nowhere near the depth of hers, but it was agony nonetheless. They seemed to be comforting each other.

Her breathing evened out, and she leaned back to look up at him. "I'm terribly sorry. How unprofessional of me." When she tried to step away, he resisted letting her go. His mission was to find the answers. When had he turned from a ruthless interrogator into a man who cared about how someone felt? He dropped his hands, releasing her.

She returned to the wingback chair, and he sat down on the couch again. Why he wanted to be close to her, he couldn't say.

When she'd finally recovered, she continued recalling the

events. "The SEAL team had been unsuccessful in finding al-Jamil, and they were ordered in as clean up…and to take credit for eliminating all of those weapons and ammunition. Since it was a completely covert operation, no one could know it was us."

Matt had read that part in the files. He also knew that they found absolutely no trace of Mason Sinclair, not a single ounce of DNA. "So, let me get this clear in my head. Gabriel Davis was in charge of the operation on site. What was Logan Jackson and Micah Reid doing?"

"Logan was the team's sniper and Micah was his spotter. They were on high ground about six hundred yards away." She seemed to have herself under control better with these questions, but he certainly missed having her in his arms.

"So, you and Teagan were the ones placing the charges?" He was simply confirming the information he'd read.

"Yes. We had trained for hours on placing the C-4 and where it would do the most damage." She leaned forward and took hold of his hands as though to emphasize her answer. "We did everything right. Every single one of our charges were assembled correctly. I have no idea how one could have gone off early."

Her silver-gray eyes were so earnest as she insisted on this fact.

He believed her. "So, you think there was a problem with one of the charges Mason planted?" Then it dawned on him. "What was Gabriel doing during this timeframe?"

Elizabeth stared at him blankly. "I don't know. He was never part of our training. He met us at the landing zone and showed us where to go. I truly don't know where he was." She stared off into space for a moment before her gaze met his. "The four of us all went into the building through the front door. Mason was on point, which wasn't the way we had practiced, but he'd insisted on setting the charges the farthest away." She blinked rapidly, obviously fighting the onslaught of more tears. "He was just trying to help us, so we could finish faster and get out of there sooner."

He was looking down the barrel of a rifle as he entered the old wooden door to a hallway. A killing zone. Fast scan left to right, up and down, finger poised to shoot. Clear. With silent steps, knees bent, he signaled to the next person to take the doorway on the left, he had the right covered. Someone squeezed his shoulder. The message was received. He stepped forward and fell into a hole in the worn boards that wasn't there a second ago.

"Another headache?" Elizabeth's gentle voice brought him back to the present.

Fuck. A daytime dream.

Matt shook his head as though to loosen the vision's hold on him. His gaze met hers.

"Who came out of the building first?" His headache was increasing. If it kept up, he would ask Elizabeth for another ibuprofen.

"Teagan finished first, and I exited right behind her." She paused and looked deep in thought. "I never saw Gabriel come out the front door, but he was with us when the building exploded." She grabbed his hands once again. He looked down where soft white hands gripped his. When had he let go of her? During the dream? Then he remembered rubbing his temples. He wasn't going insane. He could remember through the pain.

"Matthew, he saved my life." She squeezed his hands with force. "When I started to run back for Mason, Gabriel caught me, and threw his body over mine to protect me."

Another piece of new information.

"Were the communication units working?" he asked.

"Yes." She shrugged. "I think so. It was a long time ago."

"Think hard, Lizzie, it's important." He needed her to recall every detail she could.

Visibly, she fought to remember as she stared at nothing on the other side of the living room. Suddenly her hands went cold and limp. She slowly turned her head to face him. "What did you just call me?"

"Elizabeth," he said with confidence. Didn't he?

She looked at him questioningly. "Are you sure?" She tilted her head. "I would have sworn you called me Lizzie. No one has called me by that name in ten years."

He paused, wondering if he had called her Lizzie. "I apologize if I did, but the name seems to fit you."

She blinked hard to whisk away the tears, but one escaped and trickled down her cheek. He wanted to lean over and kiss it away. Instead, he used his thumb to wipe it off. Her face was so soft. He wasn't sure why it surprised him, but it did.

Rolling her luscious lips inside, she seemed to drag in one breath after another, but her gaze never left his. Finally, she was able to say, "Mason used to call me that. He was the only one." She sucked in another breath and let it out slowly. "See, my name, Elizabeth, is a family thing. My mother is also named Elizabeth, and everyone calls her Bet. My grandmother is also Elizabeth. But everyone calls her Liz. My daughter's name is Elizabeth and we call her Liza. For some reason, everyone calls me Elizabeth, no nickname. Everyone, that is, except Mason. He always called me Lizzie."

Matthew felt like a total creep. "I had no idea."

She patted his hand. "It's okay. I'm fine with you using it."

Relief washed through him and settled in his heart. It was as though she had granted him a very special gift, one that he would treasure. "Call me Matt, in that case. I think we've moved pretty far beyond Senior Special Agent St. Clare."

She tilted her head in that way she did when considering. "No, you're Matthew. I like that name in its entirety."

Whatever. "Everyone else calls me Matt, but feel free to

use whatever name you wish." *Just keep using it. I like the way you say it. Maybe, too much.*

When he gave her hands a gentle squeeze, they both looked down to where they had been holding hands this entire time. It hadn't felt awkward at all. Matter of fact, it had felt nice.

Matt caught sight of his watch. Time was slipping away from them. "I'm going to press you on this point, do you recall Mason talking to you, or base, or anyone else during the op?"

"I…I just can't be sure." She glanced away and shook her head. "I'm sorry, I just don't remember." Then she quickly added, "Sometimes when I go to bed thinking about a problem I'll wake up with the answer. If that happens, can I call you?"

The image of Elizabeth crawling into bed shot heat through his body pushing all the blood to his cock. Fucking great. Now he had a hard on. What the hell was up with that? He wasn't a horny twentysomething who couldn't control his own body, he was fifty-two years old for Christ's sake.

Then the other shoe dropped. Elizabeth wanted to call him. "Certainly." He didn't want to let go of her hands, and definitely didn't want to reach into his back pocket for a business card exposing his crotch. "I'll be sure to give you one of my cards before I leave. I'll give you my personal cell phone number. It's better we don't talk about this at the office."

"I completely understand." She glanced at the clock. "I'm terribly sorry, but I don't dare be late for my meeting." She smiled as she stood. "You know Gabriel, if you're not—"

They finish the sentence together. "Five minutes early then you're already late." They both laughed.

He delighted in her light giggle. Matthew couldn't

remember the last time he'd spontaneously laughed. It had to have been years. He couldn't even remember the situation, but he would remember every second of this one.

"Matthew, I'm terribly sorry. I seem to be constantly shoving you out the door." She glanced at his chest. "Oh, dear, my mascara ran all over your clean shirt. Let me get something to try to clean it off."

He looked at the black smudges over his heart, proud that she was comfortable enough with him to cry in his arms. He wanted to wear them as badge of honor. "No worries. I picked up my laundry on the way here. I can change in the car."

"You will do no such thing. I insist you let me clean it." She tilted her head toward the door. "Go to your car and grab a clean shirt. You can change in the powder room while I freshen my face." She pointed to the hall just off the living room. "First door on the left. Just let yourself back in. I'll meet you back here in five minutes." After issuing him orders, she walked in the opposite direction toward what he knew was the master bedroom.

He normally disliked bossy women, but for some reason, he thought she was cute ordering him around. As he bounced down the front steps, he wondered if she took charge in the bedroom as well. He preferred a woman who knew what she wanted, what she needed, and he took direction very well. He also liked being in charge, telling a woman what he wanted and exactly how he liked it. At his age, sex was all about quality, not quantity, although he didn't have any problem in that department either.

He'd enjoyed holding her way too much. His dick hadn't reacted to a woman so quickly in years. He wondered what it was about Lizzie that had turned him on so fast. He opened the passenger door of his silver Mercedes convertible and reached inside to the small backseat for a folded shirt wrapped in tissue. He was taking the shirts to the office where he sometimes changed twice a day. Going from an intense situation in the operations command center to a briefing with one of the directors, he often took a few minutes to shower and change clothes.

As he walked back to the house and jogged up the steps, the idea of stripping off his shirt and dressing in her home suddenly felt extremely personal. He couldn't count the number of times he'd done exactly that in a hotel room as he watched a satisfied woman sleep on the bed, but this was Lizzie's home. He felt intrusive, but he wasn't about to show up at the office, already late, with mascara stains on a crisp white shirt. He didn't want to give Gabe any reason to question him.

Inside the designated bathroom, Matt quickly stripped off his shirt without unbuttoning it. Tearing away the tissue, removing the collar cardboard they always slid over the top button and working in each small button through the slot took more time than he realized.

"Matthew?" Lizzie's voice seemed melodic.

He shoved his arms down the stiff sleeves and heard his name again. Without thinking, he opened the bathroom door and stepped one foot into the hall. "I'm almost ready."

Elizabeth stared at him, her jaw lax.

He knew he had a good body, especially for a man his age. He worked hard every day to stay in shape. As he maneuvered tiny buttons through the small slits over the light dusting of still dark hair on his chest, he couldn't stop the grin. She liked what she saw. And so did he.

Makeup repaired, she looked...perfect. No one would be able to tell that she had been crying. In her gray pinstripe pant suit and lighter gray silky blouse, she looked both feminine and the ultimate professional. He liked the fact that she didn't have a stick figure. No. She was rounded in all the right places. Even though her blouse was loose fitting, he would take bets that she was a thirty-six C cup. He was a breast man and rarely wrong. He'd also bet they were real. He appreciated the way her waist tucked in a little before it rounded over her hips. He preferred a woman who carried her weight proportionately over toned muscles rather than a bony figure.

He had more than his share of women and didn't bother with the young, skinny ones trying to look like movie stars rather than be who they were. They were usually lousy in bed too. Their breasts were almost always too small or, all too often, fake. There was rarely anything soft about them, including their personality. He knew what he wanted in a woman and she was standing in front of him.

Continuing to fasten his shirt, he watched her eyes drop with every button until he reached the bottom of the tails, his hands an inch away from his growing cock. He needed to unzip his pants and tuck his shirt in. Although tempted, because it certainly wasn't the first time she'd ever seen a man get dressed, he decided not to shock the poor woman anymore, today.

"I'll be finished in just another minute." He gave her his best warm smile and stepped back into the bathroom.

When he emerged into the hallway, shirt tucked neatly into his trousers, his suit jacket was conveniently draped over his arm at waist height, covering the partial erection. He had balled up the stained shirt and carried it in the other hand, so he wouldn't be tempted to touch her again.

"I'll take that." She moved toward him and reached for the shirt.

"No, you won't." He pulled it up next to his body. "It'll go with my other dirty shirts to the dry cleaner."

"No, please," she protested. "I'm the one who got

mascara all over it, and I should be the one responsible for the cleaning."

Matt was well aware of how much, or how little, Elizabeth made compared to him. She was now the sole support for her two children. She'd need every dime she made.

Changing the subject, he asked, "What are your plans for this weekend?" He headed for the front door, keeping the shirt out of her reach.

"Oh." She sounded surprised by the question. "Well, Austin has a birthday party most of the afternoon on Saturday. I thought I'd use the time to do a little car shopping." She reached for the door at the same time he did. Grinning, she allowed him to open it while she punched in the security code. "Although I've looked online, I am a touch-and-feel person. I need to see the vehicle, sit in it, drive it, before I'm willing to spend hundreds of dollars every month in payments."

He stepped through, allowing her to lock the door. "What kind of car are you looking for?" His gaze went to the sleek, expensive convertible sitting in her driveway next to the blue, four-door rental sedan.

"One that's a real bargain." She turned around and giggled. "Definitely not one like that."

They descended the steps side by side. "Do you need some help? I'm an expert at buying cars." He grinned. "I buy and sell them all the time."

She seemed to think about his offer for a few minutes before she stopped, staring at the rental car. "I hate to car shop." She fisted her hands and punched her hips. "Those damn car salesmen always try to ignore me or it's the opposite, they're glued to my side. Then they try to add on all these extra charges. If I point out the error, I'm a bitch. If I try to negotiate, I'm a bitch. I have to watch my money right now, but I need a safe and reliable car. This one has to go back to the rental agency in just a few days."

Transferring the shirt to his other hand, he touched her arm. "I know I've put you through a lot this past week. Let me make it up to you. Allow me help you find a good, safe vehicle at a fair price." He chuckled. "I can't guarantee a bargain, though. Those are few and far between."

She glanced at the rental then at him. "Okay. I'd appreciate that." She opened her car door. "Matthew, I'm sorry—"

He put two of his fingers over her lips. "Don't worry about the shirt. Let's get to work before Gabriel writes us both up." He turned to leave and remembered they needed to exchange phone numbers. "Hand me your phone."

"Why? Isn't yours working?" She handed it to him.

After calling himself, his phone rang in his pocket. He answered to establish the connection. A minute later he handed hers back. "There. I'm in your phone as Matthew." He turned his around and showed her the name Lizzie. "Text me what time on Saturday and which dealership to meet you. I'll see you then."

He slid into his car and headed to work, whistling a tune he didn't recognize. He had a date with Lizzie Kamp. Kind of. He was going to see her again and wouldn't be asking her work-related questions. He counted the hours until Saturday afternoon.

CHAPTER NINE

"Mommy, it's too hot." Liza tugged on Elizabeth's hand as they walked around the used car lot at the Chevy dealership. She had already stopped by the Ford lot and sure enough, she'd been completely ignored while husband and wife teams had been met as soon as they'd parked. She had even walked inside to ask about an SUV and had been promised, by three different salesmen, that somebody would get to her in just a minute. Frustrated after waiting twenty, she had hopped back into the rental car and driven to the next dealership down the street.

Car shopping would be easy. All the dealerships lined both sides of the four-lane highway. If she couldn't find a car there, she would never find one.

She and Liza had strolled the lot, peering in the windows of locked cars for less than a minute before a short balding man with a huge smile approached them. When she had insisted they were just looking at this point, he had followed about five feet behind them like a lost puppy until someone new parked in a customer space. She had finally given in and texted Matthew the name of the dealership.

As cars and trucks pulled into the lot, she kept an eye out for his cute little convertible.

"Lizzie."

At the sound of her nickname she froze. Chills ran through her entire body. A vision of Mason coming up behind her, grabbing her around the waist, and pulling her back to his chest blinked through her mind. Although the voice wasn't quite right, the inflection was perfect. But it wasn't Mason, it was Matthew.

She turned to watch his long, lanky body saunter toward her. Damn. He looked so good in the comfortable jeans, yellow polo shirt, and broken-in black cowboy boots. She didn't hold back her smile. "Matthew, thank you for coming." She wanted to hug him the way she would Logan or Micah, but they weren't that close of friends, yet.

When he reached her, he bent in and kissed her temple as though they were more than relative acquaintances. "It's part of the show," he reassured her in a whisper. Then he crouched down and sat on his heels. "You must be Liza." He held out his hand, and to Elizabeth's shock, her normally shy daughter took it and shook like an adult.

"I'm Elizabeth Ann Vatucci, but you can call me Liza like everybody else 'cause Mom is Elizabeth, too, and Grammy's real name is Elizabeth. I 'pose I have to name my baby girl Elizabeth. It's a family thing."

Matthew smiled at her daughter's adorable explanation. Elizabeth wished she could see his eyes, but once again, they were hidden behind the reflective aviator sunglasses.

"It's important to keep up family traditions." He looked at her in all seriousness.

"You got family *taditions*?" Liza's innocent question made Elizabeth want to cringe.

She instantly kneeled beside her daughter. "Remember

our talk about what we can ask other people? Was that on the list?"

Her daughter shook her fine blond curls. "No, Momma." Then she quickly added, "I want to know his *taditions*. What does his family make him do?"

Both Elizabeth and Matthew burst out laughing. Liza got scared and stepped into her mother's arms. "It's okay, sweetie." Elizabeth stood up holding her daughter.

"It's fine for you to ask me that question." Matthew ran his index finger down Liza's nose. "But I don't have any family traditions. I don't have any family. There's just me."

"You don't got a daddy, either? Mine's dead. He's never coming home ever again." Liza's unemotional statement of the obvious gripped Elizabeth by the throat. This was the first time her daughter had mentioned her father. Heat built up behind her eyes, not for the loss of her husband, but for everything the little girl in her arms had suffered.

Elizabeth was surprised when she looked down and watched Matthew rub her daughter's back. He was so gentle and kind with her that it touched something deep inside. No man had ever treated her children with such kindness, not even Robert.

"But you at least have a mommy. Both my mother and father are gone." Matthew's confession hit her in the same spot that Liza had just touched. She suddenly realized how very little she knew about the man next to her.

"Well, sir, I'm glad to see you could make it. That's one beautiful little daughter you have there." The smarmy used car salesman had reappeared, his gaze nailed to Matthew. He held his hand out to shake but Matthew ignored it, and him.

"Lizzie, have you seen anything on this a lot that interests you?" His focus was completely on her.

She glanced around before returning her gaze to him. "There was a four-door Tahoe that I saw online, but I haven't seen it here. On the other hand, we just arrived a few minutes before you did."

They both scanned the rows of vehicles, and in sync, stared at the salesman.

"If you are referring to the red Tahoe with the oversized mud tires and winch on the front, it is right over here." He headed to the left side of the lot.

Matthew raised his eyebrows. "Is that the one you were considering?"

"No. The one I saw was blue, or maybe black, about five years old." She started toward a line of SUVs. "It was a decent price but had high mileage." She couldn't pull it up on her phone while carrying Liza.

They stopped at the first Tahoe. This one was only a year old with high mileage. She looked down the body and it was very wavy. It had most likely been in an accident and the repair shop sucked, or the owners pocketed the insurance money and had the lowest bidder do the work. It was too much money anyway.

The next was school bus yellow. Hard pass on that one.

Matthew followed her without a word. When she came to a dark blue one, she set Liza down and read the window sticker. "This may be the one I looked at." She pulled out her phone and started punching buttons.

"There you are," the pesky salesman called from twenty feet away. "Tahoe is one of Chevy's best models. Would you like to see the engine, mister... I don't believe I got your name." He made a beeline for Matthew who continued to ignore the man. "Would you like to see under the hood?"

Matthew just looked at her. She wouldn't have a clue what she was looking at except she could identify certain engine parts. They'd studied tanks at West Point, and she knew a few engine components.

Leaning close to Matthew, she quietly asked, "Would you

be able to identify problems just by looking at the engine? I certainly can't."

"Hell, no. I have a mechanic I trust who checks out all my cars before I buy them." He stared at her a long second. "We can take yours there too before you actually buy it."

"They allow that?" She had no idea dealerships let other mechanics check out cars for potential buyers.

He grinned. "If they want to sell the car they will. If they refuse, then they're afraid of what my guy will find. I wouldn't let you buy the car in that case."

He was already invaluable. She showed him the information provided online and double checked the VIN number to be sure it was the same vehicle. "What do you think?"

"This is an excellent SUV and priced right." The salesman opened the driver's door.

Elizabeth was smacked in the face with the smell of stale smoke and wet dog. She coughed.

"How about a test drive?" He shoved the key toward Matthew.

"She's the one buying the car." Matthew grabbed the salesman's wrist and guided it to her.

"Mommy, this car smells funny." Liza crinkled her nose.

Elizabeth stepped back. "No, sweetie, this car stinks." She grabbed Liza's hand and continued to back away. "Do you have anything else in this price range that's family friendly? I have two children and I want something with a good safety rating."

The salesman looked insulted. "Ma'am, I assure you, all of our vehicles have been rated by the Insurance Institute. They are all child safe."

"I want to go. I'm hungry." Liza wound up for a meltdown.

Elizabeth exchanged a look with Matthew who started

punching buttons on his phone. When his eyes widened, she knew something was up.

Matt glared at the salesman. "That's not true. This four-door Tahoe has not been rated by the Insurance Institute for Highway Safety."

Liza patted her thigh. "Mommy, I hungry." Her poor daughter was hot and overdue for her afternoon snack. Then it would be naptime.

She picked up her tired little girl and slid Matthew a glance. "I'm sorry but I think I'd better go."

"I think we should go, too. Lizzie, I don't believe this misogynistic ass is ever going to talk directly to you, so cutting a deal on any car on this lot is out of the question. You don't need to put up with this denigration. We'll find you a car." He stared at the salesman. "One that has verified ratings."

Matthew plucked Liza from her arms. "Tell me, little princess, do you like ice cream? I feel like we all need ice cream. It's hot out here."

Liza immediately perked up. "Can I get strawberry?"

"You can get any kind you want." He then grabbed Elizabeth's hand and walked to her car. "There's a cold stone style ice cream shop about a mile down on the right. I'll follow you there." He then handed her Liza and strode to a Land Rover several spaces away.

How many vehicles does this man have? And did he just call that salesman an ass? She could have handled that slimy jerk, but liked being defended, just this once.

She strapped her daughter into the car seat.

Five minutes later, she pulled into the crowded shopping strip lot. She'd never been to this chain. Dessert was a real treat for her kids and a mid-day sugary snack was even more rare.

Matthew met her at her car and patiently waited while

she unbuckled Liza. When they started toward the ice cream shop, Elizabeth automatically took Liza's hand.

The little girl reached up and grabbed Matthew's huge paw. "We have to hold hands in a parking lot. I'm too little. Cars can't see me."

He shook his head as though in amazement. "You're absolutely right. Good thing I'm big. Cars can't miss me."

As they stepped into line, Liza ran to the case, but it was too tall for her to see.

"Do you mind—" Elizabeth started to ask him if he would wait in line while she dealt with Liza.

"I've got her." Matthew lifted her daughter under her arms, a bit awkwardly, but enough for her to see the choices inside. A father stepped up beside him with a little boy planted on his hip. Matthew immediately swung Liza up to his side, and she threw her little legs around his waist as though she'd been doing it all her life. He carried her from freezer to freezer having a serious discussion about flavors. They stopped in between two of the cases to watch a server use paddles to combine white chocolate mousse ice cream with gummy bears and peanut butter pieces. Liza's eyes were huge as she stared at the process.

Elizabeth stepped forward. They were next. "Have you two decided?"

Matthew brought her daughter back to her side. "So, what is it going to be, princess?"

Just as Liza started naming off a long list of add-ins, it was their turn to order.

"I like strawberry best, but that would be yucky with Gummy Bears, so can I have chocolate and M&Ms in mine? And can I get 'nola in it too?" At a raised eyebrow from her mother, Liza added, "Please."

The patient young girl at the register looked pleadingly at

Elizabeth. "Granola. And you can put some in my chocolate as well. I'll pass on the candy, though."

"Both you girls are chocoholics I see," Matt teased. "I'm a fan of butter pecan myself." Matt put Liza down and had the bill paid before Elizabeth could find her wallet buried deep in her purse.

"You didn't need to do that," she scolded him as they moved over to the frozen marble slab to watch the mixing show.

"I know, but since it was my suggestion, I pay." He lifted Liza back onto his hip so she had a great view.

Liza received her cone first and immediately started licking, but she couldn't keep up with the dripping mess. Out of habit, Elizabeth had grabbed extra napkins and tried to catch a drop before it hit Matthew's shirt. Too late.

"I'm so sorry." She dabbed at the spot. She hoped it would come out.

"Don't worry about it." Matt handed her the cup of chocolate and granola. "Why don't you go find us a table. Mine should be ready in a second."

When she reached for Liza, her daughter leaned into Matt. "I watching."

"I've got her." Then he turned his attention to Liza. "We've got this handled, right?"

"Right." Another drop of liquid chocolate fell onto his shoulder.

Elizabeth cringed. At this rate she'd end up buying Matthew a drawer full of new shirts.

As soon as they all sat down, Elizabeth wiped Liza's face and hands and licked the cone so it wouldn't drip for at least a few minutes.

"Exactly what are you looking for in a vehicle?" Matthew asked between bites.

"Something that's safe. D.C. drivers are crazy. The

beltway seems more like a bumper car race every day." She gave him her budget, and he nodded.

"Let me put out some feelers and see what I can find for you." He scraped the bottom of his bowl.

"Thank you for the offer, but I really can't let you do that." He was such a sweet man, but she wasn't sure what she wanted. She'd know when she saw it.

"You won't mind if I ask a few friends to keep an eye out will you?" He wiped his lips with a napkin and then handed one to Liza.

Her baby girl mimicked his movements. She could be so precious one minute and a holy terror the next. Elizabeth was pleased that her angelic child was sitting at the table. She wasn't looking forward to the sugar crash, and hoped they'd make it home first. "We need to go. Someone needs a N.A.P." Thankfully Liza hadn't caught on to that particular spelling.

After collecting all the trash they'd made, including a mountain of chocolate covered napkins, the three of them headed for the door.

"Thank you so much for coming out today." She grasped Liza's hand and headed toward the car.

He took the child's other hand. "It was my pleasure. It's not often I get to spend a few hours with two beautiful girls and eat ice cream."

When they reached the car, Liza opened the back door by herself. "Bye, Mr. Matthew." She threw her tiny arms around his thigh. His expression was comical, as though he didn't know what to do with the small person attached to him.

Elizabeth reached down. "Time to go, Liza." Reluctantly the little girl let loose of his leg and climbed into the backseat.

When Elizabeth stood after buckling her daughter in, she realized Matthew had been appreciating the view of her backside. Part of her wanted to be upset while the other part was thankful that a man still found her physically appealing. She had missed that in the last several years of her relationship with Robert.

"Thank you again for coming out today and for telling that creepy salesman off." She wasn't sure why she did it, but she went up on her toes and kissed his cheek. "And thanks for taking us out for ice cream. I haven't done that in years."

"I know you have to return this car in a few days. Are you sure you don't mind if I ask my mechanic about a dependable family car?"

She would be thrilled to death if she never had to walk on another car lot again. "That would be wonderful. You have my number if you find something." She would also be scouring the Internet tonight after both children were in bed.

"I'll be talking to you soon." He stepped away and put his hands in his pockets. "Drive safely."

She had a smile on her face as she exited the parking lot. She was looking forward to talking to Matthew again.

Two days later, her phone rang while she was on her way home from work. She pressed the button on the steering wheel to answer the call and wasn't that a delight. Her old car didn't have hands-free mode but since the rental was practically new, it had all the newest amenities, including caller ID.

"Hello, Matthew." She smiled from the inside out.

"Lizzie, I think I've found a good vehicle for you. You sound like you're on your way home. Is there any chance you can meet me at my mechanic's shop?"

She checked the time. Liza was still at day care and they were open for another hour. Austin had gone home with a friend to practice baseball since his Little League team wasn't doing well. "I have about thirty minutes I can spare."

The address he gave her wasn't far and thanks to the in-dash GPS system routing her around traffic, she made it there in five minutes. Too bad she had to give up all those luxuries within days.

She pulled in next to Matthew's convertible with the top down. He'd obviously been enjoying the early May sunshine. Smiling as she got out of the car, she looked around and spotted him talking with a man in blue overalls.

Matthew put his hand at the small of her back as soon as she approached. "Lizzie, this is my mechanic friend, George. I think we've found a car for you." Thank goodness her body knew to extend her hand because her brain had fogged over from the second he'd touched her. Familiar heat rushed through her veins, warming her heart to the man beside her.

They walked into one of the cleanest garages she'd ever seen. One of those crossover vehicles was up on a lift and they strolled right under it.

"This Chevy Equinox has an excellent safety record. I wanted to show you underneath so you can see for yourself that there isn't any rust from salted winter roads." They all stepped to the side and George hit a lever. "Whoever owned this took really good care of it." Together they walked the exterior, and he pointed out a few door dings and offered the name of a friend who did body work if she wanted to get them repaired.

"My cars live in parking lots, whether I'm at work or the store. It'll have a dozen more by the end of the year...if I buy it." She was impressed so far, but he hadn't mentioned a price. "What year is this?"

George opened the driver's door for her. "Get in and turn it on. As you can see, it only has twenty thousand miles on it."

She did as ordered. The dash lit up like a cockpit. "It has a navigation system," she announced before she could hold in her excitement.

"And that's a backup camera as well." George got into the passenger seat as Matthew crawled into the back seat.

"I'm a big guy and there is plenty of room back here." He turned and checked out the rear space. "You could carry a month's worth of groceries in the back."

Elizabeth loved this car. The black and tan leather was beautiful and would be easier to clean than upholstery. "What year is this again?" She was sure he'd never answered the last time she asked.

"It's two years old, but don't worry. I can make you a really good deal on it." George hurried to say the last sentence.

She hadn't researched this model or that year. They were out of her price range, especially since every time she turned around she discovered more bills Robert had left for her to pay and the insurance money was almost gone. "It would have to be for me to afford this car." But she really liked it.

"Take it for a drive, Lizzie." Matthew smiled at her through the rear-view mirror.

Fifteen minutes later, she was the owner of an Equinox... at an unbelievable price. Matthew had stood back and let her do everything, including negotiate the price. He'd come through for her. No man had done that in a long, long time. She was no fragile flower that needed constant tending nor special care, but truly appreciated it when someone recognized her for who and what she was. He understood her. He got her. She really liked that.

CHAPTER TEN

Mid-May

Matthew was swamped at work the entire next week. He had spent more than one night in the employee sleeping facility. A SOG team had tracked one of the top five on the Most Wanted List to Indonesia, only to lose him in the jungle. The logistics of that operation had been a nightmare.

With three days in a row off, Matt slept almost fifteen hours straight. He had been too tired to even dream, or at least remember if he had. But he did wake up with Elizabeth on his mind. In his line of work, breakfast for supper was not unusual. While scarfing down homemade pancakes drowned in real maple syrup, he'd built up the nerve to call Elizabeth.

And wasn't that a joke in and of itself. He had no problems facing down some of the most dangerous men in the world, but calling a woman on the phone and asking her out made him sweat. He never had this problem with any woman before and truly didn't understand why calling Elizabeth had become his huge mountain to hurtle.

She represented goodness and he was one of the worst bad boys on this planet. She was a good mother, had obviously been a wonderful and forgiving wife. He was a man whore who fucked whenever he wanted not caring about the woman beyond the few hours he'd spent with her. His job was killing, and he was damn good at it. Even though he no longer pulled the trigger, he was as responsible for each death as the SOG agent who released the bullet.

In the hours since he had awakened alone, he had piled the mountain of reasons that he should walk away from Elizabeth and leave her alone. But he couldn't. He was almost afraid that if he didn't discover their connection, he was doomed to sweet dreams featuring her kisses, her body, her loving words that inevitably turned into realistic nightmares jolting him awake every night with his heart erratically pounding and sweat seeping from every pore.

No. She had the answers and he was going to discover why she haunted his dreams. Before he changed his mind and thought of ten more reasons not to call her, he pulled out his phone and found her name in his contacts. Something made him glance up at the time. It was shortly after nine o'clock at night. She'd be up. He placed the call.

"Hello, Matthew." The timber of her voice went straight to his cock. He could hear the smile as she said, "I love the car. I can't thank you enough."

That was the response he had hoped for when he'd convinced his mechanic to buy the car in his name and sell it to Lizzie. Matt had given George the money after finding the safest car possible. Since he knew her budget, he made sure she didn't exceed that amount, even though he had to take a loss. He wanted to be sure she and the children were safe. Liza was such a beautiful little girl with a heart of gold. He needed to do whatever he could to protect that child.

Pictures of the demolished van that had killed her father

ran like a PowerPoint presentation in his mind. Even if the precious preschooler had been strapped into her car seat, she couldn't have lived through the crash. The very thought of losing her squeezed his heart.

Austin would have been in the shotgun seat. He wouldn't have made it either, especially as the van flipped onto that side. Although he'd never met the boy in person, he'd seen him at the cemetery and pictures of him each time he'd visited Lizzie's home. Matthew felt the same protectiveness for the young boy.

There was no logical reason for Matthew to feel this way and it confused him. He normally didn't like children, especially small ones. Gabe's kids had been little more than irritating rug rats when he'd been invited over to watch the football game. Brad was okay, but he was older and into sports.

Matthew had never felt the need to keep any children safe before Lizzie's.

"I'm glad you like it." He wasn't sure why, but he asked, "Were you able to sell your husband's sports car?"

Elizabeth laughed but there was no humor in it. "No. He didn't own the car. I found out it was leased. Just another one of the unfortunate surprises that seem to continually pop up."

"Lizzie, is there anything I can do to help you?" He worried that perhaps her financial problems went far beyond the car.

"Thanks for the offer, Matthew. You're so sweet." She sighed. "I guess I'd never realized what separate lives Robert and I had been leading for the past several years. We were more like roommates than husband and wife." She gasped. "I'm sorry, I shouldn't be telling you things like that."

"Those are exactly the kinds of things friends tell each other. I'm here for you, Lizzie. I'm happy to listen or offer a shoulder to cry on." He was surprised he meant it. If being a friend to her was what it took to understand why she had appeared in his dreams for years, then that's what he would do. He was a patient man, and all he could do was let the dreams play themselves out in real life. Hopefully, he would be able to stop everything before it turned into the nightmare.

"It's getting late, Lizzie, and I'm sure you have to go to work tomorrow. I'm off the next few days. I have a personal project I'm working on, but I'm here for you. Please, don't hesitate to call me if you need anything." He emphasized the last word hoping she understood that he would be there to help her, no matter the circumstance.

"Thank you, Matthew. You're a good friend. Good night." She sounded so tired.

"Good night, Lizzie." He pressed the button to end the call.

Since it was morning to him, he pulled out the special computer and decided to look into the life of Mason Sinclair. Matt was pretty sure he knew all the gory details about the man's death.

He wasn't quite good enough to the break into the CIA files, though. He still needed Clarence to help with those, and what a treasure trove they turned out to be.

Elizabeth had been translating Nassar al Jamil's conversations for years. From what he had read, Matt couldn't figure out why the man wasn't on the top ten list. He had been building an army for over a decade, accumulating everything from helicopters to surface to air missiles. It was as though he had a fairy godmother in the US government him.

Twenty minutes later, Matt was proud of his developing hacker skills. He'd discovered that Sinclair was one of four children raised on a ranch in Texas. His older brother,

Kenneth, seemed to have been their father's partner ever since he graduated from University of Texas. Married, with two children in college and one finishing high school next year. Financially he did better than most farmers.

Mason had a brother three years younger. Currently thirty-nine years old, Jeffery was an attorney and lived less than an hour away from their parents with his wife and four children.

It looked as though his sister, Erin, was somewhat of a whoops baby. At thirty-two, she was a large animal veterinarian and a knockout. Matt stared at her college graduation picture. Yes, she was beautiful in the girl-next-door kind of way. He suddenly wanted to pound any man who treated her badly. She'd been through enough in her life, losing a brother at such a young age.

Matt yawned and stretched. He would give this search a few more minutes. He was curious about Mason's parents. The farm had always been successful. None of the children had to take out loans for their college education, although each had received several scholarships. Smart kids.

His parents, Katherine and Dean, had grown up in the same farming community, attended high school together, and took one trip a year for exactly one week. They seemed to like the beach, although it varied each year. His mother had obviously discovered Facebook and selfies about three years ago. There were dozens of pictures of everyone in the family. He stopped and stared at a picture of Austin. Everyone around the young boy seemed happy and the child wore a huge grin. And by the looks of things, Austin visited his grandparents every summer and occasionally in between.

More tired than he had expected and finding the ever-present dull headache had morphed into jackhammering, he decided to pop a few heavy duty aspirin and go to bed.

The scene that played out in his head seemed so real he

could feel the warmth of love mixed with the annoyance of a six-year-old little girl as he took her hand and walked the long driveway to the two-story sprawling ranch house. She yammered on about her teacher and some boy eating boogers at school that day. He couldn't wait until he had enough money saved up to buy a car and be able to drive to school the way Kenneth had at sixteen. He missed his older brother even though he wouldn't admit it to anyone.

On some level, Matthew realized that was a new dream. As it pushed one, so was the next.

The little girl was a few years older and stood crying in a yellow dress. His mother held him as tears streamed down her sunbaked cheeks. Dean Sinclair blinked rapidly under the worn green ball cap emblazoned with a tractor. Kenneth was taking him to the airport. He was headed for his first summer training in the army.

Mud everywhere. Even though he had buttoned up his collar, slimy brown dirt was shoved down his chest with every thrust forward. Special Forces training was far from fun, but he could do this.

The unique smell of an excited female filled his nostrils. Bare thighs were spread as he feasted on the wet pink folds before him. Her entire body shook with need. He looked up and satisfaction filled him. He'd done this to her. To Elizabeth.

"I want you inside me, now." He loved her demands.

He loved her. As he slid into her tight heat, he told her. "I love you so much." He pumped into her as they both drew closer to that edge of ecstasy. Her vaginal wall gripped his cock and squeezed him. She was about to come and he was close...

But the darkness that overtook him was not from an orgasm. Someone had pushed him into the hole in the wooden floor.

"No. I can't die like this. She needs me."

Matt awoke to his own screams. "She needs me."

He was panting so hard he could hardly breathe. The sheets were soaked in sweat. The dream had been so vivid. He had felt every emotion from the love of a sibling to the love of a good woman. The tears his parents had shed gripped his heart. No. And they weren't his parents, they were Mason Sinclair's parents. Yet, Matt had felt every second of anguish, every moment of accomplishment, every emotion that Mason Sinclair had experienced.

Matt controlled his breathing until his heart rate settled. He stripped the bed and started the washing machine before he trotted back to the bathroom and stepped into a hot shower.

So much about the dream was disturbing. Elizabeth was younger than now so what he'd seen was the past, not the future.

Was he supposed to find out what happened to Mason? Or was he going crazy? Over a woman.

Something wasn't right about Mason's death. Where was Gabe just before the explosion?

Who wanted to kill Robert? But it was Elizabeth's car. Then does someone want to kill Lizzie?

He would kill anyone who tried to kill his Lizzie.

"This better be important, Gabriel. I have a meeting with the director in five minutes." The man pinned the throwaway cell phone between his shoulder and his ear.

"It is, or I wouldn't have called on this line." Gabriel Davis sounded curt. *How dare that little prick talk to me in that tone of voice.*

Then Gabe dropped the other shoe. "Elizabeth Kamp is becoming a problem."

Rather than roll his eyes, he just closed them and shook his head. "There is no fucking way I'm ever going to approve Nassar al Jamil onto the Most Wanted List. I can justify that up-and-down Congressional Hill without any problem. You need to make her understand that point."

"Sir, that's not the problem. I've got that one handled. He's taken a personal interest in her." Gabriel didn't have to clarify who *he* was.

Matthew St. Clare was pivotal to both their futures, and the man behind the mahogany desk understood that fact better than anyone else. "Define personal."

"He practically bought her a fucking car." Gabriel sighed heavily. "She needed a new one after hers was destroyed in the accident."

Anger boiled from within the man. "If it had been her in that car, we wouldn't be having this conversation."

"It wasn't my men who fucked that up." Gabriel's tone struck him raw.

The man chuckled. "He won't make that mistake again." Or any other. His body was buried where no one will ever find him, right beside the other men who missed their targets. "I've got this handled. Is he showing any more signs of memory recovery?"

"I don't think so. He hasn't said anything that would lead me to believe his memory was returning." Leather creaking could be heard through the connection.

Perhaps keeping Gabriel Davis in place was the better choice. He still had his uses. "It's been long enough since the last attempt. I'll put a new team on it."

"I'll continue to keep an eye on St. Clare," Gabriel promised.

The man shoved the burner phone into his pocket and

made a mental note to check all of his hidden accounts. Plan B, if this all went to hell, started in the Caribbean. He'd get a brand-new face, just like St. Clare. Then he could disappear anywhere in the world with a new identity.

He reconsidered for a moment. That might not be a bad Plan A. He'd made plenty of enemies over his thirty years of service with the CIA. God, or the devil, only knew who was after him.

Gathering the papers he'd need to brief his boss, he walked out of the executive office and down the hall.

CHAPTER ELEVEN

"Knock, knock. It's me."

Elizabeth instantly recognized the voice of Teagan Williams. "Come on in. I'm at the dining room table." She had been expecting her best friend for nearly an hour, so she had unlocked the front door and released the security system.

"What the hell is all that?" Teagan walked to the wet bar and retrieved an open bottle of white wine. Grabbing two glasses, she brought everything to the dining room table. "You look like you could use this as much as me."

Elizabeth sighed as her gaze perused the foot-deep piles of paper. "You have no idea." She held out her hand all but begging for the glass of crisp white wine. "It's been three months since Robert died and I still keep finding bills." She rubbed the spot in the middle of her forehead. "I'm so distracted by all this shit, I almost got hit by a car last week walking into the grocery store."

"What the hell?" Teagan picked up a pile of papers from one of the chairs and found enough open space on the table to set them. "Some bitch almost ran you over?"

"No, I think it was a man, but I really couldn't tell. The windows in the van were almost black." She sipped the wine and savored the flavor as it crossed her tongue. "If I didn't know better, I'd think he was coming right at me. I jumped between two parked cars to get out of his way. I swear he came within an inch of one of the bumpers."

"Did you at least get his license number and report him to the police?" Teagan's suggestion made sense.

"No. I was much more concerned about getting the shopping done and through the checkout line in less than thirty minutes, so I wouldn't be late, again, for picking up Liza." She glanced at the papers. "To be honest, I didn't even look for a license plate number. I'm sure the driver was just distracted. Probably calling his wife to make sure he'd gotten everything on her list."

"You're probably right." Teagan looked around. "Where is everybody?"

"Austin is in Texas visiting his grandparents and cousins and Liza is at a play date three doors down." Elizabeth looked at her watch. "I have about an hour before I'm expected to get her. In the meantime, I'm stuck with all this." She threw her hands up. "We had separate accounts our entire marriage, and a joint account for all household expenses. I can't even figure out how much money Robert made or where he spent it. Nothing here balances."

Teagan's gaze slowly swept the table. "I don't mean to get personal, but without Robert's assistance, can you make the mortgage payment on this place?" A second later she added, "And still eat?"

"That's exactly what I'm trying to figure out." Elizabeth slumped back in her chair and took a large drink of wine. "We had an insurance policy that should've paid off the house, except Robert had taken out a second mortgage, without my consent I may add. The insurance paid off the remaining balance of the original loan, but the second one wasn't covered."

"Who the fuck gave him a second mortgage without your signature? I didn't think that was legal in the state of Virginia." Teagan's eyes flashed with anger.

Elizabeth's blood started to boil, again. She had been furious when the local branch manager informed her that the second mortgage did not carry an insurance policy, only the first, and that she was responsible for the remaining balance. "According to the leading loan officer in this region, and yes, I went over the local branch manager's head, Robert had his own personal banker. Very personal. Who is no longer with the bank, by the way."

"So, this bitch arranged a second mortgage on your house without your knowledge?" Teagan clarified.

"Yes, and the loan officer even admitted that the entire circumstance was highly unusual but assured me everything was legal." Elizabeth leaned forward and put her elbows on the table. "Then the son of a bitch had the gall to tell me the exact date the next payment is due." She threw her hands up in the air. "From what I can tell, Robert had been making that second mortgage payment as a deduction from his personal account, so there was no chance I would ever find out about it. All correspondence about it went straight to his office."

"That sucks." Teagan leaned forward with her elbows on the table. "I have a friend who is a forensic accountant. Why don't you let me take all of this to him? He was a genius with my mom's stuff. He actually found some accounts and investments that my father had. Mom had lost track of so much by the time I finally got out of the Navy."

"How is your mom doing?" Elizabeth felt terrible for

Teagan. She had wanted a career as a Navy pilot, but when her father passed away suddenly, she discovered that her mother was in early stages of Alzheimer's. As soon as her contract was up, she moved back home and took a job as a civilian at the Pentagon.

"Same shit different day." She gulped her wine. "Some days she remembers me, other days she thinks I'm a housekeeper. I can't tell you how many times I have heard the same stories. That's why I love coming over here. New and different things happen to you. My life is exactly the same every day."

"Who are you dating now?" For years, Elizabeth had lived vicariously through Teagan's love life wanting more from her own relationship with her husband.

"I wouldn't call it dating." Teagan poured herself another glass of wine and topped off Elizabeth's. "To me, dating would include going out for food, maybe even a nice restaurant every once in a while, taking in a movie, or cuddling on the couch watching a movie. All Brandon wants to do is fuck. He doesn't even come over for dinner anymore. He says Mom stares at him. He waits until she's gone to bed then texts me to see if I want him to come over. Lately, we head straight to the bedroom. I certainly can't complain about anything he does in there. The man is good. He always leaves me satisfied and sleeping. Dating? No. I think were both just a booty call for each other."

"At least you're getting some. I haven't experienced the big O in..." Elizabeth really had to think about it. "Anniversary. We'd gone out to dinner to celebrate our fifth anniversary. It was almost as though it was obligatory sex. I'm not sure either of us was really into it." She'd known even before then that her marriage was in trouble. She really wondered, especially lately, what she'd seen in Robert.

"So, when are you getting back into the dating game?" Teagan deflected the attention back onto her.

Elizabeth instantly thought of the handsome man with white hair and a black mustache. Her salacious thoughts went to his ripped body, and, damn, the man was fine.

"What's that smile for?" Teagan stared at her for a moment. "There's a man in your life," she accused.

Matthew St. Clare's gorgeous face popped into her mind. Heat rose up her neck and her face.

"Oh. My. God. You do have a man." Teagan leaned forward, elbows on the table. "Were you seeing him before Robert…died?"

"No. I…" Elizabeth was taken back for a moment when she realized she had met Matthew at Robert's funeral. "Do you remember the white-haired man with the black mustache that came to the cemetery with Gabriel?"

"Oh, most definitely." Teagan smiled. "That man was delicious. Under that custom-tailored suit, he had a set of shoulders on him that were drool worthy."

Elizabeth had seen those shoulders up close and personal. She had cried on them as he had held her in his strong arms. "I've…" She couldn't tell anyone why Matthew St. Clare had been to her house several times. "I've seen him around couple times. He helped me find my new car."

"That was nice of him." Her friend stared her down. "What aren't you telling me?"

"You know how you can't tell me exactly what it is that you do with the Pentagon? All I know is that you work for five of the highest-ranking women in the military on a special project." Elizabeth was on a roll. "Well, I can't tell you why Matthew St. Clare came to this house a few days after we buried Robert."

She then smiled. "But I can tell you he brought over pizza

last week because I told him I was running the kids everywhere and didn't have time to cook supper. Then, when Austin stormed into the house complaining how he was the worst player on his Little League team—he'd missed a grounder and the other team won—Matthew took him into the backyard and threw the ball with him for about an hour."

This next part was harder to share. Teagan didn't have children and Elizabeth didn't know if her friend would understand. "When they came back in, they were both laughing." She rolled her lips in so her chin wouldn't quiver. "Teagan, I can't remember the last time I heard Austin laugh. I didn't realize my son was so miserable."

Teagan got up and came around and kneeled beside her. She threw her arms around Elizabeth. "He wasn't the only one who was miserable. I hated seeing you become the recluse you were with Robert. Please don't take this wrong, but I'm glad he's gone and out of your life. You have the opportunity to start fresh. You're only forty-two years old. You can't let that bastard ruin the rest of your life. You deserve happiness which means you deserve a man who makes you happy."

Tears had started to stream down Elizabeth's cheeks. "Robert has only been gone three months. I have no business thinking about another man."

Teagan laughed. "You have every right to think about another man. Ten minutes ago, you confessed to me that it has been nearly a year since you had sex." She grinned. "Sex with a partner."

That made Elizabeth laugh and cry at the same time, mostly because it was true. If it weren't for her battery-operated boyfriend, she'd be beyond sexually frustrated.

"Now, how soon are you going to jump what's-his-names' bones?" Teagan was teasing, or at least Elizabeth hoped she was. Although her relationship with Robert had been estranged for a long time, hooking up with the first man who came along had never been a consideration. But maybe it should be.

"I don't really know when I'm going to see him again, but I can assure you I'm not going to sleep with him then." She reached for her wine to fortify herself.

"With Austin in Texas, you can't use him as an excuse to have Matthew back over to help him with his baseball. You know, it's perfectly okay for you to call him and ask him out on a date. Women do that all the time now," Teagan pointed out.

That wasn't a bad idea. "Austin will be back next week. He'd asked Matthew to help him with his batting, but he'd had to cancel because he was going out of town on a business trip at the last minute. I'll bet he'd be willing to work with Austin as soon as he gets home."

"Okay, that gets him here in the house, but that doesn't get the two of you alone." Teagan went to the frig and foraged for some cheese. Grabbing a small cutting board and a knife on her way back, she set them on the table.

"Oh, we've been alone before. He came over for supper the night before Matthew left. We stayed up for hours talking after the kids went to bed." Elizabeth smiled. "He helped me with the dishes. I'm not even sure Robert knew we had a dishwasher. Matthew is such a nice guy. I don't know what to do with a nice guy."

"Sure you do. Mason was one of the best men I ever knew." Teagan found a box of crackers in the pantry and brought them back to the table. "Grab those sticky notes and those clips. I'm taking all this with me and giving it to my friend. You're going to let him sort it out."

Ten minutes later, Teagan stood at the door with two boxes of files. "What other loose ends do you need tied off?"

Wow. Elizabeth had to think for a second about that one.

"I closed the account where Robert did his banking and paid off the damn credit card that I didn't know a fucking thing about, but I still need to clean out the safe deposit box he had there."

"When do you want to go?" Teagan's straightforward, no-nonsense attitude was one of the reasons they were great friends.

"That bank isn't open on weekends, so we'll have to do it one day during lunch." Elizabeth couldn't figure out any other time that would work.

Teagan lit up with happiness. "I love getting out of the office for lunch. Thanks for the excuse but let me check my calendar."

She opened the door for her friend and gave her a one-armed hug. "Call me next week."

Halfway down the stairs, Teagan turned and smiled. "You better call me if you wind up with a date with Mr. Hottie. I expect complete details."

Elizabeth laughed. "Don't expect much."

She checked her watch. She still had thirty minutes before she needed to go pick up Liza. Relief washed over her as she looked at the nearly empty dining room table. The few remaining piles, and her life, seemed manageable.

The boxes stacked in the corner caught her eye. She had methodically gone through room by room, closet by closet, removing Robert from the house and her life. She'd kept a few photographs of Robert for Liza. There may come a day in her life when she would like to see what her father looked like. Those were set aside to eventually be placed into a photo album. With only half an hour, Elizabeth decided to tackle the master bedroom closet. Grabbing an empty box, she headed to the room she once shared with her husband. Her gaze swept the large walk-in. Robert's clothes had occupied the left half, which was now nearly empty.

A few days after his passing, she couldn't stand looking at his clothes every time she stepped in to grab a clean suit for work. She tossed his neatly hung dress pants, suit jackets, starched shirts, and ten pair of nearly new shoes into a garbage bag and dropped it off at a thrift store. She probably could have made a couple hundred bucks by selling each item at a consignment shop, but Elizabeth didn't even want to touch his clothes ever again.

As she stood hands on hips surveying the rods and shelves, there really wasn't much left. Golf shoes, that were so clean they were either new or seldom used, went into the box. A pair of running shoes that looked older than their marriage, got tossed in the garbage.

She found the stepstool so she could get the sweaters off the top shelf. No one probably needed them this time of year, but she would take them to the thrift store anyway. Not caring, she tossed several stacks of sweaters, ski clothes, and polar fleece pullover's to the floor. As she moved the last stack of turtlenecks, she froze.

Elizabeth couldn't breathe. The brown wooden box with intricate carvings sat tucked into the corner. She dropped everything in her hands and slowly reached for the familiar chest. She picked it up as though it were made of eggshells.

It still smelled like Iraq.

She sat down on the stepstool and stared at the complicated hand carved design. Eight sided stars, semicircles, overlaid squares, filled every square inch of the top. She ran her fingertips over the carvings, remembering the day she and Mason had strolled through the small village open air market. Although they weren't on duty, they wore helmets, flak jackets, and tan desert boots, casually carrying semi-automatic rifles. For that hour they were just a man and woman enjoying the day together. Always alert, of course. ISIS was everywhere.

Displayed on a handmade Persian rug, the boxes had caught her eye. She looked at several before negotiating the price. Before she could dig out her money though, Mason had already paid for it. The box was the first gift he'd ever given her.

Fighting tears, Elizabeth took several deep breaths. She couldn't open the box. It would be too painful.

She'd already lifted the lid.

The small slips of paper were already yellowing at the edges. Maybe she should take them out and preserve them with thermal film. She discarded the thought as she touched the first note.

Think of me because I'm thinking of you.

She ran her finger over the familiar handwriting then picked up the next one.

I love you. Always.

The feel of the paper, knowing Mason had touched it, made her miss him once again. He was really a romantic at heart. When they'd go out on missions separately, he'd write her little notes and stuff them into her pockets. She'd find them at the oddest times, always at the perfect moment. She plucked out another one.

Look for Orion tonight. I will too.

On clear nights, especially when they were out on maneuvers where the sky was so black and the stars so bright, they would find a minute or two to share the constellations. Mason always found Orion first, but she could pick out Pegasus in any sky.

A warm tear dripped onto her hand. She ignored it and picked up the next small piece of fragile paper.

I will always love you.

Elizabeth's phone buzzed, notifying her that it was time to pick up Liza.

She wiped her tears and headed for the front door. She

was halfway across the living room before she realized she was still holding the box. She set it down on one of the end tables and headed out the door. She needed to hug her children. She couldn't wait for Austin get back home and hold him.

CHAPTER TWELVE

Matthew sat next to Gabriel at a well-worn rectangular conference table. The Pentagon reserved the inlaid oak tables and swiveling executive chairs for dignitaries and members of Congress. Even though there were six flag officers in the room with multiple stars on their shoulders, they were sequestered in the basement for security reasons.

Army General Lyon, the new commanding officer of Special Operations Command, most often referred to as USSOCOM, was being briefed about high priority targets in the Middle East. The new general—who was ultimately responsible for all Navy SEALs, Army Special Forces, and the Marine Corps Special Operations Command—did not want his teams tripping all over the CIA's Special Operations Group.

Everyone understood they had to work together quite often with the military taking the credit for eliminating some of the worst men on the planet. Almost always though, it was CIA intelligence and the SOG teams who worked directly for Gabriel at the Special Activities Division who actually hunted down these criminals. Since SOG teams never wore any kind of insignia, or even a uniform unless it was a disguise, and always worked covertly, the new general was attempting to establish better communications between his command and the CIA.

It seemed reasonable, and on paper looked doable, but Matthew knew better than most that in the field, communication could often be tenuous. His gaze slid down the table.

The representative from the National Security Agency didn't look like he even owned a pair of hiking boots and had never laced combat boots halfway up his calf. The looks the generals exchanged every time he spoke was comical.

For hours they had worked their way through everyone's list of top ten most wanted in each volatile area of the world. They had left the Middle East for last. Although most could agree on the top five, there were fifteen more names batted about.

"I think we need to take a harder look at Nassar al Jamil," suggested the admiral from Naval Special Warfare Command. "He's a sneaky bastard. Our information suggests that he's been building an army for years, buying everything from tanks to rifles from the Russians or anyone else who would sell them to him."

"He's a small wannabe with delusions of grandeur." Gabe scoffed. "Our research indicates that he would like to set himself up as the next caliphate, but he doesn't seem to be gaining any traction. He keeps getting kicked out of country after country. The only thing he seems to keep gaining is wives. Our reports indicate he might be a little too fundamentalist."

"Like he doesn't already have enough women to fuck?" Came from somebody a few chairs down. Several people near Matt chuckled quietly.

"He is off the list," announced General Lyon.

The meeting droned on for another hour before he and Gabriel were able to escape.

"I have an extra ticket to the National's game on Saturday. You interested in joining me?" Gabriel asked as they hiked to his agency car. Matthew loved baseball, and everyone knew it. Normally, he would jump at the chance to go watch a professional game. He liked Gabe, not just as his boss, but as a friend. But Matthew had plans on Saturday.

"Sorry, I promised Lizzie that I would work with Austin on his batting." Matt had never forgotten Gabe's warning all those months ago. Nor could he forget the first time he'd ever seen Lizzie. Even the professional suit couldn't hide her gorgeous body.

Gabe stopped midstride. "Lizzie? Do you mean Elizabeth Kamp? Please tell me you're not dating her."

"I wouldn't say I'm dating her. I'm helping her son with baseball." *And giving Elizabeth time after her husband's death before I actually do start to date her.*

"How did you end up coaching Austin?" Gabe studied Matt's face.

Becoming a great liar was actually a class at the CIA. Matthew had spent several years in the field under cover, so he was an expert. It was always best to stay as close to the truth as possible when telling a lie. "Elizabeth and I ran into each other and started talking. At some point she mentioned her son played baseball." Matthew smiled. "What she really said, was that he was one of the worst players on the team." He shrugged and started walking toward the car again. "The kid doesn't have a father any longer, so I volunteered to help." Matthew was quite sure Robert had never played baseball, or any other sport, with his step son. The one time he'd tossed the ball with the bright boy, the kid had eaten up the attention. He was a quick learner, listening to instructions and willing to try until he got it.

Matt was quite excited when Lizzie had called and asked him to come over two days after Austin returned from Texas visiting his grandparents. Matt now knew them to be good people, thanks to his research. Hopefully, after he and Austin worked on his batting, he could take them all out to dinner. Like a good friend.

"Elizabeth has been through a lot." Gabe slid in behind the wheel. "She's not your usual type, and by that, I mean fast and fun." He stared at Matthew before turning the key. "We've been friends a long time, and I've never known you to keep a woman past the two-week mark since that plastic surgeon."

Gabe was correct. Matthew didn't do relationships. And yes, Lizzie was different. There had been something there from the start. He didn't believe in love at first sight, that was just ridiculous, but he could admit to having a spark with one or two women. With Lizzie, it was a blowtorch.

"Maybe I just haven't found the right woman, yet." Matt decided to turn the tables. "I guess I'm just not as lucky as you to have found the love of my life three times. By the way, how is the hunt for Mrs. Davis number four going?"

The edges of Gabriel's mouth turned down as he put the car in drive, heading back to Langley. "I really did love them all, you know. I will always love Janie as the mother of my first son. It's really too bad she couldn't handle the life of an agent. I spent twice as many days away from home as I did with her when Brad was little." He smiled, but it might've been a sneer. "Lacey," he said her name on a sigh, "she was everything Janie wasn't. She had to be one of the most beautiful women I've ever known, fun and exciting all the time...on the outside. Inside, she was the most self-centered, money-sucking bitch I've ever had the misfortune of marrying." Gabe slid him a glance. "But you know all that. Did I ever thank you for being by my side during the ugly divorce? Damn, that woman was relentless."

"Yes, you usually thanked me about halfway through a bottle of Jack." Matthew smiled. "I'm just glad you listened to me about ditsy Kitsy. That woman was fucking crazy, and I knew it the first time I met her."

Both men laughed.

"But Christ, that woman could give head." Gabe maneuvered onto the beltway.

"The problem is, no matter how good they are in bed, unless you leave in the middle of the night, you have to talk to them in the morning," Matt pointed out. "I just haven't found the woman I wanted to talk to after morning sex."

Gabe was silent for several minutes. "Marsha and I used to talk for an hour every morning while drinking coffee and having breakfast. Then we had kids and our entire world changed." After several more minutes of silence, he added, "Do you think I'd be crazy to call Marsha and ask her out for coffee?"

"Do you still love her?" Matt knew the answer to that question but hoped Gabe did too. His friend talked about their two kids almost every day. He was such a proud father. But that wasn't enough to hold his marriage together, although Matt didn't know the exact reason they had separated three months ago. It wasn't any of his business.

Matthew thought about the coffee idea a moment as he considered Lizzie's mornings. "You could be a really thoughtful guy and bring her Starbucks coffee. Maybe even show up early and make the entire family breakfast." He glanced over at Gabe. "I know for a fact you're pretty good in the kitchen."

Gabe's grin grew. "That's one hell of an idea."

Matt thought so too. Maybe one day soon he'd show up and make breakfast for Lizzie's whole family.

Four hours later, Matthew pitched the ball to Austin. "Don't try to hit it, just watch it the entire way as it goes by." The boy did exactly as asked.

"Excellent. Now toss the ball back to me." It landed with a thud in his well-oiled glove. "Good throw." Austin stood taller at the complement. The boy just needed some confidence and practice. His hand eye coordination was quite good.

As Matt squeezed the ball, he noticed it was softer than it should be. It was old. He noticed earlier that Austin's glove was a little on the small side for him. He was a growing boy and no doubt needed a bigger size.

"Okay, Austin, this time I want you to hit the ball. Remember the box. I promise, I'll throw it so you can hit it." Five seconds later the crack of the bat connecting with the ball thrilled Matthew more than if he'd personally hit a homerun. "That was absolutely perfect."

Matthew ran to the makeshift home plate and hugged Austin. "Great job."

"I did it! I really did it." Austin was jumping up and down in Matthew's arms. "Can we do that again?"

Matthew smiled into the overjoyed young face. As it always did when he looked at Austin, the familiar warmth spread through his whole body. He never thought he liked kids before, but he really enjoyed his time with this boy. "We sure can."

After jogging back to the pitcher's mound, he lobbied the ball over home plate. Austin connected with the next pitch. Matt reached up and grabbed it as it flew over the pitcher's mound. As the boy continued to connect with the ball, Matt started throwing real pitches; fastball, curveball, even a slider. Austin got them all.

He still needed a lot of practice, but at least he had the basics of batting down pat an hour later when Lizzie stepped onto the back deck. She took his breath away. She was beautiful in jeans and a loose-fitting blouse with light makeup.

"I was thinking about ordering Chinese," she announced. "What would you like?"

Austin trotted up next to him and Matt automatically threw his arm around the young man's shoulders. "Did you see what your boy did?"

His mother beamed. "I sure did. I am so proud of you." She held Matthew's gaze. "I can't thank you enough for taking time to help Austin."

He gave the boy a hard half hug and released him to his mother. "I really enjoyed this," Matthew admitted. "As for Chinese, I'd rather take you all out to dinner to celebrate how well Austin did today."

The boy's eyes went big. "Can we go, Mom? Please. It's been so long since we've gone out to dinner."

Matthew wondered just how tight money was for Lizzie, but he would never ask. "There's a Chinese place in the mall at Tysons Corner." He grabbed Austin's glove and flipped it toward him. "Put this on." The boy immediately slid his fingers into the leather glove. Matthew felt how tight it fit and knew he needed a new one. "I want to congratulate Austin with a, new glove. This one is too small. We might want to pick up some baseballs while we're there, too."

Lizzie would be a terrible poker player, he concluded. Her face showed every emotion and worry was written over every feature.

Matt smiled broadly. "Tonight is my treat." He held Lizzie's gaze. "Please, let me do this for him, and you."

An hour later Matthew was positive he'd made the right choice. The all-you-can-eat Asian buffet was a winner. Liza could flat put down some shrimp and the girl liked it cooked every way possible. She scooped up popcorn shrimp with a spoon, decided she really liked crab stuffed butterfly shrimp that was deep-fried, devoured a shrimp eggroll, and still had room for shrimp lo mein. Austin made three trips, piling food high each time and cleaning the plate. Lizzie had chosen to create her own combination while Matthew hit the sushi bar.

Stuffed, everyone headed into the mall. First stop was the sporting goods store. For a nine-year-old, Austin was very price conscious. Matthew had selected a high-quality glove but one look at the price tag and the boy had set it down. He'd tried on several, checking the tag each time. "I think this one fits." He flexed his fingers, but it wasn't near the quality of the one Matthew had initially selected.

Kneeling, to be on the same height as Austin, Matthew held both gloves side-by-side. "Usually, you pick the glove best suited for your position, but on your team, positions are rotated. So that makes it a little tougher for us to decide what kind of glove you need. The one you picked has very long fingers, which is perfect for an outfielder. Infielders use smaller shorter gloves with the shallow pocket so they can grab that ball out of there and throw it fast to get the guy out at first base."

Austin nodded. The child seemed to be absorbing every word and nuance. Damn, he liked this kid. He truly wanted to learn, had wonderful manners, and a good soul. He just needed a male role model in his life. Not for the first time, Matthew wondered what kind of relationship Austin had with his stepfather.

Refocusing on baseball, he pointed out the pocket-size, webbing, and padding and compared adjustments. Matt had selected a traditional all leather glove for its durability while the one Austin had chosen was synthetic. "I want you to be as safe out there as possible, so you can play your best game every time. You're not going to want to catch a ball if you know it can hurt your hand."

"Mr. Matt, thanks for wanting to get me a good glove, but I can't let you spend this much money on just baseball." He pointed to the tag. "That's a whole lot of money."

The fist that tightened around Matt's throat was nearly as strong as the one grabbing his heart. He raised Austin's chin until their eyes met. "You are worth every dime."

The child blinked rapidly, then he threw himself into Matthew's arms and hugged his neck tight. "Thank you, Mr. Matt. Thank you." He whispered in his ear as he sniffed back tears.

Matt rubbed the boy's back. "I just want you to be safe and have fun. Do you like playing baseball?"

Sniff. "I do now. I used to suck at the game and get yelled at a lot. Now that you've been helping me the coach says I'm getting good." He leaned back and looked Matthew in the eyes. "I can get even better, though, now that I have a really good glove." He tore away from Matt with the biggest smile he'd ever seen on the child. "Mom. Look at my cool glove."

Matt took a deep breath and sighed. He had just lost a chunk of his heart to that little boy. Standing, he needed to go find Elizabeth and Liza. He was smart enough to know he couldn't buy one child something special and not the other. What the hell did four-year-old little girls like? Besides ice cream, which was a great idea for their next stop.

Half an hour later, faces cleaned of all traces of ice cream, Matthew carefully watched Liza as they walked back down the mall toward the exit nearest where they'd parked. The little girl had slowed so much in front of the doll store that Lizzie finally bent and picked her up, carrying her away from the storefront filled with lifelike dolls and giggling little girls around the table that looked like a birthday party. Liza's birthday was coming up, according to his research. Maybe he would take her there to select her own doll. Then they passed a store where children could choose a stuffed animal, select the clothes and shoes and even the noises it made. Perhaps Liza would like that better.

Elizabeth made a beeline for a small corner store filled with costume jewelry and mothers with small daughters. It took ten minutes to guide Liza around the store as Matthew and Austin hung out in the back corner. He had carefully watched Liza's eyes grow big as she played with a fuzzy covered purse. When Elizabeth glanced down at the price, then redirected her daughter's attention elsewhere, Matt knew the handbag was out of the price range.

"Come on, Austin, I want to get something special for Liza too." Matt grabbed the fuzzy purple purse and was checked out before Elizabeth even knew they had moved.

Ten minutes later, they finally left the store and headed for the car. "Mr. Matthew, do you like my bracelets?" Smiling ear to ear, Liza stuck her arm out for him to see the half-dozen colorful plastic bracelets.

"They're gorgeous, just like you." She was such a cute little kid. "You know what you need to make your outfit perfect though?" He handed her the bag. "Every woman needs a purse."

Matthew's complete attention was on the kids and not his surroundings when Lizzie shoved both children at him. "Protect them," she ordered as she stepped toward a man in a leather jacket, just as he thrust a knife toward Lizzie.

CHAPTER THIRTEEN

Something about the man walking toward her had caught her attention. He was staring directly at her. His dark brown skin and nearly black curly hair had thrown her back to her Army days in the Middle East. She dropped her gaze over his body searching for weapons. Her blood ran cold at the flash of the six-inch blade.

Her maternal instincts took precedent over everything else, so she had shoved the children toward Matthew. He was more than capable of protecting them while she eliminated the threat.

As the man entered the lethal zone, within contact range, his hand was far enough away from his body as he prepared to thrust out his arm to jab the knife into her. She twisted before releasing a sidekick to knock the knife out of his hand. Grabbing his wrist and using her continual momentum, she flipped the man onto the hard floor. He *umfed* as his spine met cold tile. His wrist still clamped in her hand, she flipped him over onto his belly. After kicking his legs apart, she stuffed her knee next to his balls. Leaning against his most vulnerable spot, she grabbed his other hand, bending his elbows and held them both at the middle of his back.

"Don't touch that knife," she ordered no one in particular. "I need handcuffs." Her eyes never left the man sprawled on the floor under her as he bucked to get free.

"Don't even think about moving." Matthew was three feet away with a gun pointed at the man's head. They were locked in a stare down. Her children were tucked behind him. Definitely safe. "Somebody give her a pair of handcuffs." His voice boomed across the gathering crowd.

"Sir, I need you to put that gun away." A skinny man in a tan uniform came barging through the gathering crowd.

"I'm senior Special Agent Matthew St. Clare, and there's no way in hell I'm taking my loaded weapon off this perpetrator until he's in handcuffs."

"But...but...I'm John Kaplan, the head of mall security tonight, so in this mall I'm in charge." The man's voice was slightly shaky at first but grew stronger. "You need to put that gun away."

"Well, John, do you have a pair of handcuffs that you can give to Agent Kamp so she can secure the prisoner?" Matthew sounded a little irked.

"Uh...no," the mall cop said quietly. "They don't let us have handcuffs. But I called the police. They have a station right here in the mall, you know. They're probably out on patrol but should be here any minute."

"Wonderful," Matthew said sarcastically. "Maybe one of them will have a pair of handcuffs."

The man under Elizabeth twisted as though to break free so she shoved his hands farther up his spine at the same time leaning in to pinch his balls, making him arch in pain.

"John, why don't you help out with crowd control and give us twenty feet of perimeter, but don't let anyone leave," she ordered. "They may be needed for questioning."

John's radio squawked. He answered with their location, glanced at Matthew then added, "Somebody with a badge, weapon pointed at the suspect who is detained on the ground."

A man in blue jeans and a button-down dress shirt stepped forward "I have a pair of cuffs. Agent Kamp, let me help you with that. I'm Detective Stephen Evans, D.C. Metro police." He kneeled and quickly tightened the restraints on the man.

"Let's leave him face down, I don't want him on his knees. It's too easy to run into the crowd." Matthew's gaze was darting all over the floor. "Where's the knife?"

Several teenage voices responded. "It's over here, sir."

"We didn't let anybody touch it," A young male voice called out.

"We got it all on video." The feminine voice sounded over excited.

"I'll handle it," volunteered the detective as he stood.

"John, how about that crowd control." Matthew kept his gun pointed at the man on the ground so Elizabeth felt confident about getting up. Her children needed her, and she wanted to be sure they were okay. As soon as she was several feet away from the perpetrator, both kids rushed over to her.

"Way to go, Mom. You kicked ass." Austin threw his arms around her waist while Liza clutched on tight to her leg.

"I was so scared. Mommy." When Liza started to shake, Elizabeth picked her up and turned so her daughter couldn't see the man on the floor. She moved Austin so her body blocked his view as well.

Within minutes, several members of the Fairfax County police were on site and took control of the scene. They immediately separated her from Matthew and a female police officer took charge of her children. The woman must've had kids herself, or was well-trained, because she was extremely good with Liza and kept them within sight of her.

When the police read the perpetrator his rights, he hadn't said a single word. One of the officers tried to question him, and all he did was stare silently at Elizabeth. It really creeped her out. She heard one of the officers call in for a Spanish translator.

"Excuse me," she said to the officer who was taking his statement. In Arabic, Elizabeth asked her attacker what language he spoke. She could tell by the look in his eyes he knew exactly what she said.

"You're dead. You just don't know it yet, bitch," he answered in a familiar Arabic dialect.

Elizabeth couldn't breathe. She had thought, hoped, that she was simply a random victim of some kind of gang initiation. But no. She was a selected target.

"What did he say?" The officer questioning the perpetrator asked.

She couldn't answer. Her heart was beating so loud blood was pulsing in her ear's. Her mouth was as dry as the Iraqi desert where this man was no doubt born and raised.

"Ma'am, what language was that?" asked the officer trying to take the terrorist's statement.

Yes, at that point she knew him to be a terrorist. What she didn't understand was why he was after her. Her mind instantly went to all of the translations of the past week. None had involved a specific person, a specific target, or even the United States. Had he been here longer than a week? A month? Could he be part of a sleeper cell that has been here for years?

Someone gripped her bicep. "Ma'am, are you all right?"

She snapped out of her thoughts and focused on the police officer in front of her.

"You went white as a sheet. Do you feel ill?" Concern was

written all over the hard face of a law enforcement officer who had seen too much in his lifetime. "We can step over here and you can sit down if you'd like."

Elizabeth forced a deep breath, then another. She glanced over and gave her children what she hoped was a reassuring smile. "I'll be okay. He speaks Arabic. If I had to guess, I'd say he's from the area where Iran, Iraq, Syria, and Turkey share borders."

The officer stared at her a long moment before he replied. "That's a very specific information. You know this man?" He tilted his head toward her assailant.

"No, I've never seen him before in my life." Before he could ask, she offered, "I'm an Arabic translator for the CIA."

The officer's eyes lit up. "You know exactly what he said."

Something deep inside started to shake Elizabeth. She tried to gather what little moisture she could to swallow down the tension that filled her throat. "Yes. He told me I was dead but just didn't know it. Then he called me a vile word. In English it's similar to bitch, but in Arabic it...it..." She couldn't control the quiver in her voice. She sucked in a breath. "It's a woman who is unclean, a whore, the worst kind of woman in their religion."

Elizabeth was none of those things, and she knew it to her very soul. She didn't understand why this man thought of her that way. It hurt her. She was a good person. Even while serving her country in the Middle East, she was there trying to make things better for women and children, especially little girls. Her gaze flew to her daughter who stood holding hands with her older brother. In her other hand she carried two bags.

In silent prayer, Elizabeth thanked God for allowing her and her children to be born in the United States of America, giving women the opportunity to be anything they wanted to be thanks to free education for all.

"Agent Kamp." A new voice stole her attention. A different law enforcement officer, this one a bit older with more stripes, held out an unopened bottle of chilled water.

"Thank you." She took the bottle and immediately cracked it open, downing nearly half. "Thank you," she repeated. "I needed that more than you will ever know." She sipped.

The kind smile the new officer gave her helped her refocus. He glanced over at her children then at his watch. "I know it's getting late, and you want to get your kids home and into bed. If you will help us finish up with your statement, we can let you go." He nodded toward Matthew. "I believe Agent St. Clare has made arrangements for your assailant to be moved as soon as we can get the paperwork settled. I think we're almost finished." He looked to his officer for confirmation.

"Yes, sir. I just need her to reread her statement and sign it." Her inquisitor handed her the clipboard. She quickly read what he'd written as her explanation of events. She'd tried to be very concise and selective of her wording as though she was giving an incident briefing to a superior officer back in the Army. She signed the bottom of the sheet and thanked the officer before she went to her children.

As she hugged Liza and Austin, she watched Matthew who seemed to be more in control of the situation than any of the law enforcement officers present. Glancing over at her assailant, they now had him standing with a huge man in a blue uniform on each side. A Middle Eastern man was trying to talk to him, but he still said nothing. His glare never left Elizabeth.

Fear for the safety of the children in her arms made her break out in a cold sweat. If they knew who she was, and they were after her, they now knew about her kids. Liza and Austin were her life and she would do anything to protect them. She had worked at the CIA long enough to know what evil existed in the world. She had seen where children had been kidnapped simply to get at the parents. She would not allow that to happen to hers.

The senior ranking officer on scene approached them. "Mrs.," then he corrected himself, "Agent Kamp, may I have a word?"

They both looked at the policewoman. "We're doing just fine here." She turned, capturing Liza and Austin's attention.

Elizabeth and the officer stepped far enough away from her children, so they couldn't hear. "Since you translated what your assailant said, I don't need to tell you your life is probably in danger. There isn't much we can do to be absolutely honest with you. We can increase patrols in your area, but this guy followed you to the mall. He's probably been casing your house for days, maybe even weeks. My suggestion is that you start to vary your schedule, change up your routine, take different routes to work, and most of all, let your bosses know what's happening. The agency protects their own much better than we can." He slid a glance to the man who was being walked by his officers to the nearest exit. "Good job on taking that one down, but you might not see the next one." He held her gaze. "It's even harder to dodge bullets."

"Thank you, officer." She held out her hand and he took it. "I appreciate anything you can do." Her gaze went to her children and held there. "I know what I have to do." She forced a smile as she looked up at him. "Right now, I have two very worried, and extremely tired children. I need to get them home and into bed."

Matthew approached and put a hand at the small of her back then rubbed up and down her spine. His reassuring touch let her relax slightly. She let out a long slow breath as she dropped her shoulders.

He ignored the officer. "You okay?"

She didn't even try to hold in the smile. "Not really," she admitted. "But I'm better now that you're here. Let's go home."

"I'm ready if you are." They both looked to the senior officer.

"I don't think we're going to have any more questions for either of you, but I doubt you're finished answering them." His gaze tracked to Matthew. "We'll transfer him over to your custody as soon as we get the paperwork. I don't want him in my jail any longer than he has to stay there."

Everyone knew exactly what he meant.

"I'll do what I can to expedite the transfer." Matthew held out his hand to shake.

"We'd appreciate that." The officer nodded to each of them. "Agent Kamp. Agent St. Clare. Good luck."

Matthew pulled Elizabeth into his arms and simply held her.

Damn, she needed that; his heat surrounding her, his hand as it slowly rubbed up and down her back, soothing away the rough edges of her attack. She buried her face in his chest and smelled lingering body wash, deodorant, aftershave, Matthew, she didn't know which, but it was nice.

She knew herself, and her body, well enough to realize she was about to hit the post-adrenaline slide. Her kids would be feeling those same heightened emotions, but they wouldn't know how to deal with them. She had to get the children home, now.

As though Matthew could read her mind, he released her. "Come on. Let's get the hell out of here."

The policewoman had stayed with the children even as other law enforcement officers had left the scene.

"Thank you so much, for everything," Elizabeth said as she shook the woman's hand.

"You have great kids. They're strong, but you still might want to consider counseling. What they saw you do tonight was pretty traumatic." She gave Elizabeth a small smile. "My kids have never seen me at work. I'm not sure they would've handled it as well as yours did. Something to think about." The last, she had said to herself as she walked away.

Elizabeth picked up Liza who clung to her neck and buried her little face under her mother's chin. She was surprised when Austin reached up and grabbed Matthew's hand. Her son had never shown such affection to Robert. His response had usually been the opposite, to walk as far away from his stepfather as possible. The bond that was growing between those two touched her deep inside, and she lost another piece of her heart to the man who'd had her back two hours ago when someone tried to kill her.

Someone tried to kill her. Her skin broke out in goosebumps. She began to sweat as her heart raced.

No! The word screamed through her mind. *Breathe. You have control of your body and your mind. Set it aside until after the children are in bed. Then talk it out with Matthew.*

Both children were silent as they strapped into the backseat of Elizabeth's car, holding their bags like security blankets. She had given Matthew the keys when he quietly asked for them as they hiked through the nearly empty lot. Although she could force herself to safely drive home, it was nice to turn over that duty to someone else.

Matthew pulled into the garage and closed the door as soon as he turned the engine off. Elizabeth sat in the passenger seat and took in the now cleared space. It had been filled with Robert's stuff since he had moved in the house shortly before they'd been married. Although he had tools and a workbench, a table saw, chopping saw, a bandsaw, grinders, and so much more, she had never once seen him turn on a single machine, nor had he ever shown her anything that he had made with his own hands. She couldn't figure out what he was doing with all that carpentry equipment.

She had initially wanted to give it all to Habitat for Humanity, but the husband of one of her friends estimated the value and helped her sell every piece. With the money, she was able to make several payments on the second mortgage Robert had left her.

Rustling from the back seat brought her attention to the present. She quietly opened her door, then the one next to her sleeping daughter. As she lifted Liza into her arms, she saw that Matthew held Austin and was carrying the snoozing boy, bag clutched to his chest, into the house.

Once again, it struck her. Robert had never carried either child into their home. Yet, here was a man who had no ties to these children who was taking better care of them than their own father. How could she have stayed with him all those years? If it hadn't been for the accident—

You're dead. You just don't know it yet.

Her assailant's words came back to her.

Robert's accident.

In. Her. Car.

No! Was he dead because someone had tried to kill her and got him instead?

Her breathing had started to increase, again. It was the adrenalin letdown. She knew it.

Get Liza into her bed. Get her into her nightclothes. Tuck her in. You can do this. Just hold on.

She rushed through getting her daughter ready for bed, then peeked in to see Matthew struggling to pull a nightshirt onto Austin. Together they managed to get the boy into bed without really waking him.

Matthew led the way to the living room then helped himself to her wet bar. "Wine or something harder?"

"Hard, please. Scotch." She collapsed into one corner of the couch.

When he handed her the glass of amber liquid, he sat down right beside her. She was glad he hadn't selected a different seat.

"We really don't know each other that well, but I'd like you to stay the night." She didn't look at him but swirled the whiskey, capturing its scent with her next breath. "I'm sorry I don't have a guest bedroom, but would you mind camping out on the couch?"

He slid his arm around her shoulders and pulled her tight against his side. "You couldn't throw me out of here if you wanted." He kissed her temple, and she melted into him as relief sank all the way to her toes.

With a shaky hand she lifted the glass to her lips and sipped. The smooth burn started at the tip of her tongue washed through her mouth. She felt it all the way down as it slowly made its way to her stomach.

He sat his drink down on the coffee table in front of them then took hers from her hand and set it next to his.

Matthew leaned back into the heavily padded couch and pulled her over until they were chest to chest. "It's okay. You're safe now. Let it go."

She did.

Every ounce of tension, every drop of adrenalin, emptied from her body through her tears. He simply held her, rubbing his warm hand up and down her back, whispering reassurances.

It took a while, but she finally got control of her body once again. She didn't want to move. She liked the feel of laying against his chest, sharing her stress with him. Allowing him to help her carry the burden of the day.

Elizabeth had no concept of time. She could have cried for five minutes or fifty. When she was finally able to breathe easily again, she asked, "Did they tell you what he said to me?"

Matthew's hand stopped in the middle of her back. "Who said something to you?"

"The man who tried to stab me." She raised her head to look up at him. "I take it the officers didn't tell you what he said?"

"No." He shifted her so he could see her entire face. "What did that fucker say to you?"

She repeated his exact words in Arabic, not knowing if he was familiar with the language. Many men who were stationed in the Middle East knew a little Arabic. He certainly recognized the derogatory term.

"Would you translate for me, please? My Arabic is very rusty, and I don't want to mistake what I think he said."

"His exact words were, 'You're dead. You just don't know it yet, bitch.' At least that's the way I would have translated it if I were at work. I think we both know *bitch* isn't quite the right word, but it doesn't translate well into English."

He pulled her down to his chest and cupped the back of her head with his big hand. She fit so well in the hollow of his shoulder. "No. They can't be after you. You can't be a target. They can't take you from me, I just found you."

CHAPTER FOURTEEN

Rationally, Matthew knew Elizabeth could be a target. He just didn't want it to be true.

"First, I work for the CIA in a highly classified department. Second, I'm a translator specializing in Arabic." She gave him a raised eyebrow and damn, that was so sexy. He kind of liked her all defensive. "For the past ten years, I've been translating conversations from one of the most dangerous men in the world." Then she muttered under her breath, "Even though I can't seem to convince Gabe of that fact."

"Lizzie, it's much more likely that your affiliation with me has made you a target." His hand seemed to rub up and down her back of its own fruition, but he needed to touch her. "You know that I am the deputy director of SAD. I control more than a hundred special operators all over the world. There are dozens of powerful men who could easily threaten me by hurting you."

Fuck. This was exactly why he avoided personal relationships. He should've stayed with one-night stands. But there was something about Lizzie that seemed to attract him on a cellular level. He had given up fighting it. He only wished he understood what he was supposed to do with the information about Mason Sinclair. He truly wanted to believe they were after him not her.

"Are you kidding me?" There went that sexy eyebrow up again. "I didn't even know you when Robert was killed."

"True, but are you thinking that Robert's accident wasn't an accident?" He didn't think she knew about the brake lines.

"That's exactly what I'm beginning to think." Reaching back, she grabbed both glasses, handing him his. Obviously in need of a little liquid courage, she sipped and waited a long minute after she'd swallowed. "What if they were after me before tonight? He was driving my car because my brakes felt squishy."

Damn, he couldn't lie to her, and not telling her would be a lie of omission. "I read the police report on the accident. The brakes had been tampered with."

Her hand flew to her mouth. Her eyes filled with tears, but she was able to blink them away. "He died because of me. That was supposed to be me in that accident." Her eyes went wide then. "At that time of day, I would've had both children in the car. We would have all been killed."

Matthew didn't want to think about Liza and Austin being strapped into the backseat as that truck plowed into her old van. Or those poor children being left in the care of Elizabeth's husband. No. He would not allow his thoughts to go there. "We don't know that for sure. What we do know is that someone tried to—" Matthew couldn't say the word. "Someone attempted to stab you tonight. Your quick thinking prevented him from harming you."

Her hands flew to her mouth and terror crossed her face. "The parking lot."

"What about the parking lot?" Had someone been waiting for her after work and tried to attack her?

"I didn't think anything of it at the time. I thought perhaps he was just distracted ..." Lizzie raised her gaze to meet his. "A few weeks ago, I was coming out of the grocery store and someone in a van with blacked out windows..." She glanced away before returning her gaze to him. "If I hadn't slipped between two parked cars, they would have hit me."

Damn. That could not have been a coincidence.

"We need to deal with this situation. We have to protect both you and the children."

She threw back the rest of her scotch and set the glass on the table. "I need to find someplace safe for the children. I'm sure the Sinclair's would take them if I explained the situation. They have a really big ranch, and nobody shows up there uninvited." To herself, she added, "I wish I knew someone from Mason's old Special Forces team to go down there with the kids to protect them."

"You might want to consider asking Logan and Micah," Matthew suggested. "They might know someone who would take on a temporary job like that."

Her eyes lit up. "That's a really good idea." She reached for her phone then saw the time. "I'll call them tomorrow."

"We have to figure out how to protect you. It is getting late," Matthew reminded them both. "I'm just going to run out to the car and grab my go bag. I'll only be a moment."

Elizabeth stood and smiled. "Go bag. I haven't heard that term in seven years, nor have I needed a bag packed with everything to survive for forty-eight hours since I left the Army."

Matthew stood up. He wanted to take her in his arms and just hold her. But he needed to figure out a way to keep her safe once the children were in Texas. His home was the logical choice. He not only had an in-home security system, but his yard was rigged with the most high-tech system available. He looked into those beautiful gray eyes that were now rimmed with red. She wasn't ready to go to his house, yet.

She glanced around her pretty home. "I really like civilian life, but after tonight, I'll never leave home unarmed again." She looked up at him. "I haven't thanked you."

Her soft hands on his face surprised him, but when she leaned in and pressed her lips to his, he was almost too shocked to move. Almost. He tried to prolong the connection. It was as though he'd been waiting all his life for that kiss. The kiss was over far too soon. Matthew vowed that he would be kissing Lizzie again.

Looking a little dazed, she stepped back. "Uhm." She took another step backward. "While you…uhm…" Another step farther away from him. "You go get your bag, and…" In another step she was at the corner. "I'll…I'll grab some sheets and blankets for the couch." She disappeared down the hall.

That answered that question. She was just as affected by the kiss as he was. He smiled. Yes. He would be kissing Lizzie again soon.

From his car, Matthew grabbed his briefcase, which contained the special computer Clarence had rigged for him, as well as his go bag. Though, he wasn't sure how he was going to be able to sleep with a raging hard on. He might use the time to investigate Lizzie's assailant, or research more on Mason.

By the time he returned to the house, Lizzie met him at the door to lock it and set the alarm. She already had the couch covered with sheets and blankets and a pillow at one end for him. He made sure he kept something in front of his crotch, so she couldn't see his erection. That would be just too embarrassing, especially for a man his age.

"You know where the bathroom is." Lizzie pointed down

the hall. "I laid out a fresh set of towels for you. They're blue." She seemed very nervous.

"Thank you." He said, much preferring the way she said thank you earlier. He hadn't been prepared for that quick kiss, but he desperately wanted another. Life was too damn short not to take chances. Given the way she wouldn't look at him, the way that kiss had affected both of them, and the fact that anything could happen to either of them tomorrow, he decided to take a chance. "Lizzie, come here."

Stiffly she walked toward him. As soon as she was within reach, he took her by the shoulders and gently brought her in close. "I liked the way you said thank you, so I hope you like the way I say good night."

He lightly brushed his lips over hers then kissed the edge of her mouth before heading in the opposite direction and gently laying his lips on the other corner. As he made his way back to the center. She threw her arms around his neck and pulled him in, pressing her lips hard against his. She opened for him, and he dove into sweetness, and strangely, familiarity. They both tilted their heads in opposite directions, adjusting the angle, as though they had been kissing like this for years. She tangled her tongue with his in a sultry dance that he absolutely loved. He moved his hands down her sides and cupped that beautiful ass of hers, pressing her against his rock-hard cock.

She froze.

Damn it. He had moved too fast. He needed to take things slower.

"I'm sorry," they both said at once as each took a step back.

Lizzie was breathing hard, but she managed to say, "I... we...I'm sorry. It's the adrenalin. After a long-continued adrenalin high, the body produces high quantities of hormones including pheromones which attract the opposite sex. It's the body's way of assuring continued life." She looked up at him in all seriousness and announced, "My body wants to have sex with you."

He chuckled quietly so as not to wake the kids. "You felt the evidence that my body wants to have sex with you too."

"It's just the adrenalin," she interrupted.

He didn't even try to hold back the huge smile. She was adorable in professor mode. "I'm well aware of the aftereffects of an adrenalin high. We used to call them combat boners." He stepped closer to her.

Slowly, he reached out with one hand to cup her face. "I can guarantee you, not all of this was caused by hormones. I've wanted you for a long time, Lizzie. But, I know you're not ready yet." He leaned in and gave her a sweet slow kiss. "Good night, Lizzie."

When her gaze met his, her eyes were clear crystal with hints of blue. "I'll let you know when I'm ready." She went on tiptoes and gave him a quick kiss before turning around and heading toward the master bedroom.

Mentally, he did a fist pump. Yes. He'd have her in bed soon.

Matthew did a quick check of all the doors and windows before he headed into the hall bathroom to change into sleep pants. As he stretched out on the couch, he thought he'd try to sleep. Obviously, the day had caught up with him. By his fifth deep breath, he was pulled under.

Somewhere in Matthew's mind he knew it was just a dream, but, damn, it was a fantastic dream. He was on his back and Elizabeth was naked, laying on top of him, chest to chest, hips to hips. He could feel the heat of her center on his cock. She tore her mouth from his and kissed down his throat, over his Adam's apple and placed a small kiss in the small U of his collarbone. She didn't stop there.

Her fingers rolled his flat nipples while she continued her

journey over his tight abs. At his belly button, she followed his happy trail with her tongue.

He could feel his erection grow as the heat of her breath climbed up its length. She took just the tip into her hot mouth and swirled her tongue.

Christ, her mouth on him felt fantastic. He looked down his body to see the top of her head, and wove his fingers into her soft brown hair with streaks of blond where it had been kissed by the desert sun.

She took more of him into her mouth and wrapped her fingers tight around the base. She knew exactly how he liked it, because he had taught her what to do. She had also let him know exactly what she liked. He could still taste her orgasm ten minutes ago on his tongue.

She sucked hard as she jacked the base until he couldn't stand it anymore. "Lizzie, enough. You know I don't like to come in your mouth. Get up here and ride me."

Lifting her head, she just grinned at him. He knew that look. She was going to keep it up until he exploded inside her mouth. He much preferred to be inside her hot, wet channel. He loved the way her body gripped him, her internal muscles rippling, squeezing, and releasing his cock as she approached the edge.

"Please, I want to be inside you," he begged.

Her eyes softened. She kissed the very tip then licked the drop that had escaped his control. She kissed the spot two inches inside his hip. "You know, when I first saw your birthmark, I thought it was a tattoo. I wanted to ask you who the M K stood for, but then I realized it was a birthmark."

Matthew bolted wide awake. He started to shove down the sheets and his sleep pants, but he knew what he'd find. He had seen it a thousand times in the shower and never thought anything of it. It was just part of him and always had been...because the reddish-brown jagged lines were a birthmark inside his right hip.

None of this made sense. Was he going crazy because he had spent so many hours researching Mason Sinclair? He scoffed at that idea. Was that any crazier than considering that Mason was calling out from the dead, begging Matthew to solve his murder and vindicate him? No. Was it possible that his dreams were actually memories trying to force their way through?

Anyone who had ever seen a hypnotist in action knew the power of suggestion to the brain. He worked for the fucking CIA who were masters at training. A vision of the man lying in the hospital bed next to the psychiatrist's offices popped into his mind, except he was the man in the bed. He'd been in one of those beds, probes hooked to his head and various spots on his body, his hands tied to the side, so he couldn't rip out the earbuds or turn off the constantly playing television. He'd been in a room exactly like that one.

"He might be remembering." The psychiatrist had said those words to someone on the phone right after Matthew's psychological evaluation. He didn't think they were talking about him, but what if they were? What if the CIA had messed with his brain? Every memory seemed so real. But was it?

He touched the birthmark on the inside of his right hip. Was Matthew St. Clare really Mason Sinclair?

He needed proof. Something concrete to connect him directly to Mason Sinclair. Physically, they were the same height and similar build. And had the same birthmark. Not impossible, but highly unlikely. Their faces were different, but Matthew had undergone multiple operations after the car accident— Was there really a car accident? What else could account for all his broken bones and smashed face?

The nightmare. Him crawling out only to be smashed to pieces by falling debris.

The pain in his head was five times worse than ever before. But there was no way in hell he was going to take any of the meds prescribed by the CIA doctors. He had to work through the pain to get to the truth.

Matthew had no idea what time it was, but he got up anyway. In case the children woke up, or Lizzie wandered out, he threw on a pair of blue jeans. The house was plenty warm, probably in an effort to minimize heating and cooling bills, so he didn't bother to put on a shirt.

After firing up his computer, he checked the schedule and discovered that Clarence was also off tonight. Matthew shot the young man a private message. They had worked out a code that meant Matthew was in trouble and needed computer help. Thirty seconds later, Clarence was on the burner phone.

"How can I get into our psychological files?" Matthew said without as much as a hello.

"No problem, big guy. Standby. Logging into your computer now." The tech genius had complete control of the screen in front of Matthew as box after box popped open and closed. He was getting used to this happening, but it sure beat taking the computer back to Clarence at the office. Gabe was already too aware of everything Matt did, and he wasn't ready to answer any questions.

"You're in," Clarence declared. "That didn't take anywhere as long as I expected. They don't protect those files enough."

"Well for Christ sake, we're not going to tell them until I'm through," Matt demanded.

"Anything else you need, big guy?"

"What, you got a hot date?" Matt couldn't image the geek getting more sex than he was.

"Not to brag, but I left a warm bed and a hot woman to handle your problem. Now that I'm awake—"

"Don't say another word," he threatened. "Thanks, Clarence. I appreciate it."

"I'd appreciate a promotion and a huge raise. Can you make that happen anytime soon?" This had become a running joke between the two of them.

"Sure. Right after I'm made Director of SAD." Matthew ended the call. He had work to do.

CHAPTER FIFTEEN

Elizabeth hadn't slept well, but she'd be kidding herself if she had expected to get some serious sleep. Everything that had happened at the mall paled compared to Matthew's kisses. Knowing that he was sleeping twenty feet away, protecting her and her children, was reassuring but he'd made sure she knew he wanted her.

Visions of them together in her bed repeated over and over. The ways he'd take her. The positions she wanted him. With just a kiss, she'd been willing to invite him down the hall and into her bed. No one had ever kissed her like that before. Certainly not Robert. Mason's kisses were wonderful, but Matthew knew how to kiss and make her feel like a woman.

As soon as she'd pushed those thoughts away to concentrate on sleep, the flash of the blade aimed for her shocked her system wide awake again. It was as though she was reliving the event over and over. She commanded herself to stop that line of thought.

Rolling over to check the time on her phone, she decided it was far too early to call the Sinclairs. Even though they were ranchers and got up before dawn, she needed to wait at least another hour or two since they were in Texas and on Central Time.

Scanning through her contacts, she came across Logan's name. He'd be up. More than once he'd talked about running on Onslow Beach on Camp Lejeune and watching the sun rise. She hit the number.

"Elizabeth." Logan panted. "Are you all right?"

"No," she answered quietly. Five minutes later, she'd explained the situation. "Do you know anyone who could go to Texas and watch over the children? Keep them safe?"

"As a matter of fact, I do. It'd be good for him." Logan's breathing had slowed as though he was walking. "One of my captains was injured by an I.E.D. a few months ago on a mission in Iraq...chasing our favorite caliphate wannabe. He's doing some intensive physical therapy, but they're getting ready to release him to finish on his own. Physically, he's recovering, but mentally...he lost three good men. I think some R and R in Texas with civilians is perfect for him. I'll head him your way in a few hours. He can escort the kids to Texas and stay with them until things settle down with you. Sound like a plan?"

Elizabeth was near tears. She had the best friends ever. "That would be wonderful. I'll call the Sinclairs and let them know there will be three staying with them. What's this man's name?"

"Zeke, Captain Zeke Gates. We call him Buck. He's from farm country in Wyoming. Used to ride bulls if you can believe that." The laugh in Logan's voice was unmistakable. "A Texas farm is just what the man needs. Do they have horses?"

"Lots of them." Elizabeth loved going to the Sinclair ranch. She felt closer to Mason there, riding the same land he'd ridden as a child and staying in his childhood bedroom, although it had been remodeled. Katherine and Dean were wonderful grandparents to Austin. They were so much like her own parents. They loved each other and their children. Thank God they loved Austin as much as they did their other grandchildren. Liza had stolen their heart as well. She and Dean had a special bond, especially when it came to the animals.

"Let me see if I can get Buck on a transport flight to D.C. today." He paused. "Elizabeth, you need to be careful. Very careful."

"I–" she started to reassure him but he bowled over her.

"I know you can take care of yourself. I've fought beside you. But these sons of bitches seem determined to kill you, and it's been years since you've been in combat. Your life is different now." He breathed out audibly. "Fuck. I wish I could take off a few days and hunt these fuckers down myself, but we're chin deep in shit on several continents. I can't break away. I'd call on Micah, but he's in the same boat, and we're all sinking fast. USSOCOM has us spread so thin at the moment we're barely giving our men three months stateside before flipping them back out. I'm sorry, but I just can't leave right now."

"That's okay. Matthew is here helping me." She sounded excited because she was. Just having someone at your side was wonderful, but it was Matthew. He'd proven himself to be a true friend, and solid in a dangerous situation.

"Who the hell is Matthew?" Logan sounded warry.

"We met him the day of Robert's funeral. He was with Gabe." Had that been almost four months already? Yes. The time had flown because she'd been so busy with work, the kids finishing the school year, their sports, and Matthew. He'd become a growing part of their life.

"The old guy?" Logan spit out. "I'm not sure he'd be much good in a gunfight."

"Matthew isn't that old. I think he's in his early fifties, maybe even late forties. Neither of us has room to talk since we're only a few years younger. I think the white hair ages him." Elizabeth wasn't sure how old he was, and a few years didn't matter at their age. His face looked like he could be ten years younger than her, almost too pretty, angelic. His eyes told another story. They were hard, like they'd seen too much. He was the most handsome man she'd ever seen. And he was fit. Plus, he'd had her back last night.

She needed to change the subject. She was confident that Matthew would help her figure this out. "I have to call the airlines and make some reservations, as well as the Sinclairs. Call me when Zeke is on his way so I can make arrangements to pick him up. Thanks for everything, Logan."

"Will do. Be safe, Elizabeth." He ended the call.

She checked the time and called the Sinclairs, the airlines, and her boss. Everyone was on board. Zeke would fly with her and the children on the redeye where she'd walk them through security to meet Katherine and Dean. She'd turn around and take the next flight back. Her children needed to be as far away from her as possible.

She smelled coffee brewing and heard someone in the kitchen. Matthew. For a while, she'd forgotten about him. She quickly showered and dressed, pulling on a pair of comfortable jeans and an old Army T-shirt. Barefoot, she entered the kitchen to find Matthew in a deep discussion with her children about the blueberry pancakes he was making. She didn't know she had blueberries.

"I like it when the blueberries are in every bite." Austin poured juice into glasses as Liza set the kitchen table.

"I likes ta put the syrup just in the middle and dip each piece into the puddle." Liza set a knife down then moved it. "Where does that go?"

Matthew and Austin said at the same time, "Knife and spoon are on the right, so forks are all that's left."

"I know that, but which is my right?" Her precious daughter glared at her hands.

Elizabeth laughed out loud. "Let me help you with that, princess."

Liza pulled the silverware to her chest. "I gosta do this. Mr. Matt said that was my job. We gotta be real helpful today cuz you had a bad day yesterday with that bad man in the mall."

She wasn't sure who she wanted to hug first, her daughter or Matthew. Even though there was that kiss last night, she wasn't sure if things had changed in the light of day, or now that their bodies had dumped all that adrenalin. Then too, she wasn't about to start showing affection for a man so soon after Robert's death. She chose Liza.

Scooping up her daughter, she hugged her tight. "I love you, princess." And then she placed kisses all over her face, loving the way her baby girl laughed. When she stopped, and set Liza down, she chased Austin around the table. "Your turn."

"Really, Mom, I'm good." Austin said, smiling as he darted by her, just out of range. She finally caught her son around the waist and kissed him loudly several times on his cheeks.

"Mom, I'm not a little kid anymore," he insisted as he wiped his face with his hands.

"You will always be my little boy, and I will always love you." She released him and sensed someone watching her. Looking up, her gaze met Matthew's. His eyes were almost gold in the kitchen light. He gifted her with that small smile she was coming to like way too much. It touched something deep inside and made her nervous and anxious at the same time.

"How many pancakes will you eat?" Matthew asked.

"I'm starved. Two, please." Elizabeth decided it must be the hormonal let down, but she was really hungry.

He raised an eyebrow. "Really? You're starved and two is all you can eat?" He was teasing her, and she liked it.

Her smile was sweet as she answered, "Yeah. Two. I normally eat one and it fills me until way past lunch." The idea of meals and planning the rest of the day brought her back to reality of everything that needed to be accomplished the next few hours.

"Guess what," she announced as she wandered to the stove to see what else Matthew was cooking. "You kids are going to Texas tonight and spend some time with Katherine and Dean."

Austin ran toward her and hugged her around her waist. "I love the farm. How long can we stay? Are you going to ride the horses with me again? Maybe Liza can ride the pony." He tore away from his mother and ran to his sister. "Grandpa Dean bought a new pony for all his grandchildren. His name is Dusty, and he's all brown. We have to brush him out and curry him real good before we ride him because he likes to roll in the dust in the pasture."

"Austin, do you know why you have to brush him really well before you put a saddle on him?" Matthew asked as he put small pancakes onto a plastic plate adorned with Disney characters.

"Yeah. Because Grandpa Dean said we have to."

At her son's simple statement, Elizabeth laughed out loud. She was joined the second later by Matthew.

"Grandpa Dean can be a real stickler for the way his horses are treated." Matthew put one large pancake onto a plate then carried both to the table for Liza and Austin. "Sit down and eat before it gets cold," he ordered the children. As he returned to the stove, he explained, "If you don't get the dirt out of their coat then when you put the saddle blanket and saddle on the horse, it could rub them and they could end up with an open sore. Then nobody can ride them for weeks."

"Did you grow up with horses?" Austin dug into his pancake.

"Yes. I grew up on a ranch, if you could call it that. It wasn't much of a farm though." He dished up two more plates with two pancakes on each and brought them to the table.

"Grandpa Dean and Grandma Kate have a big ranch. They have horses, cattle, and even a bunny. They grow stuff, too." Her son filled his mouth with pancake.

"Austin. You know the rule. Nothing bigger than a quarter." He had manners, but sometimes Elizabeth needed to remind him.

After chewing the oversized mouthful, he responded, "Yes, ma'am." He sipped his juice. "This is going to be fun. All of us at the ranch."

That would be fun, thought Elizabeth, but not going to happen this time. She needed her children safe. "Just you and Liza are going. But a friend of Uncle Logan is going to go with you. His name is Zeke."

Matthew set the plate down in front of Elizabeth and held her gaze. "Logan found someone?"

She nodded up at him then continued, "We are all catching the redeye to Dallas. I'll walk you through security, like usual, but this time Liza is going to the ranch, too. Zeke is going to be with you, all the time."

"It'll be like we have a new daddy." Liza's words struck Elizabeth in the heart. Did she want a new father? Robert had hated the ranch and refused to go, even though he'd been invited. Elizabeth hadn't pushed the point because it was Mason's home. In truth, she didn't want to share that with Robert.

"No. Zeke is just a friend of Uncle Logan's." Elizabeth needed to be sure the children understood that fact. "Because of the bad man in the mall, Zeke is going to make sure there are no bad men anywhere near you."

Austin was about to put a small piece into his mouth. "Besides, if we get a new daddy it's going to be Matthew."

"What?" Both Elizabeth and Matthew said at the same time.

"Mr. Matt is going to be our new daddy. Right?" The boy bounced his hopeful gaze from Elizabeth to Matthew then back again.

Matthew just smiled at her and set his fork down on the plate as though he was curious as to how she was going to handle the question.

"Why do you think that?" Elizabeth asked her son.

The boy's eyes got large. He knew he was put on the spot. "Because he spent the night here at our house. He didn't go home like usual."

Oh, hell. Her son was far too observant. Elizabeth looked into the living room and saw no sign of the bedding she had set up for Matthew last night. Her gaze flew back to him.

He winked at her. Yes, winked. Then gave her that little half smile that melted her brain to mush. "Yes, Austin, I did spend the night here...on the couch. After what happened at the mall, I wanted to make sure everyone of you is safe."

"Cuz you got a gun to protect us." Liza pointed her fat fork toward Matthew.

"I do have a gun, and both of you know never to touch a gun, right?" Wasn't that wonderful he'd addressed that point so perfectly?

Both children nodded their heads dramatically.

"Right. But when I'm an adult I'm gonna learn to shoot so I can protect my mom and Liza." Sometimes, Austin could be the sweetest little boy. Elizabeth thought about the two pistols in small gun safes in the house. She should really have a talk with Austin about gun safety. She had grown up with weapons, had a BB gun when she was eight years old. She then remembered that Austin was nine. Perhaps for his birthday, or maybe even Christmas, she would get him his first gun. She also needed to look into gun safety classes for him.

"After breakfast we are going to go pack some clothes for both of you." She looked directly at her son. "And we're going to clean up your bedroom." She would probably have to do several loads of laundry before they had everything they needed.

"Can I take my new baseball glove and the new ball?" His pleading eyes were impossible to refuse. The dark brown and gold, just like his father's, spoke volumes without him having to say a word.

"Perhaps Grandpa Dean or your uncles will throw the ball with you." Matthew forked up a stack of pancake, dripping with maple syrup. "Your Uncle Kenneth was quite a ballplayer at one time. He played baseball in college for a few years." He set the fork down then rubbed his temples.

She was about to ask Matthew how he knew so much about the Sinclair family, but his obvious pain shoved the question right out of her mind.

"Sure, sweetie. I know you want to break your glove in," she said distractedly to her son. She redirected her attention to Matthew. "Can I get you something for the headache?"

"No, but thank you." By the way he rubbed his entire scalp, she knew he was fighting pain. Men. Why did they think they had to be so macho? All he needed to do was swallow a pill, and he'd feel better soon.

When the children were finished, Matthew volunteered to do the dishes since everyone else had lots to accomplish.

"Elizabeth, what's your flight information?" He looked past her, so she glanced the same direction. The hallway was empty since the children had gone into their bedrooms. He pulled her into his arms. "I'm not letting you out of this house alone, say nothing about traveling all the way to Texas without me."

When he brushed his lips over hers, she forgot any protest. "I'd like that." Having someone at her back made her feel so much more comfortable.

"I need to make some arrangements with the office so that the airline will know that I'm carrying a weapon. I'll also make sure we're all seated together." He ran his fingertips through her hair. Tingles started at her crown and settled between her legs.

"I would really appreciate that," she managed to say. She wanted him to touch her again, to feel like a man wanted her. She leaned in and felt his erection. Oh, God, he did want her. She swallowed hard then looked back down the hall towards the children's bedrooms. "I have a lot I need to get done today." She went up on her toes and kissed him. "Thank you for making breakfast and dealing with the dishes."

She tried to pull away, but he held her in place. Then he gave her the half grin. "I did a lot of work this morning. I think I need a better thank you." He lowered his head to hers, giving her plenty of time to back away, or run away. She wasn't going anywhere. She wrapped her arms around his neck, and leaned into him, opening her mouth right after contact. He tasted sweet like maple syrup and coffee.

"Mom, I can't find—" echoed from the hall.

Elizabeth jumped back two feet. Her fingers flew to her kiss-swollen lips. She couldn't help but look up at Matthews eyes which had turned nearly golden.

"I'm coming," she called over her shoulder then rattled off the flight information as she headed to get her children packed.

As she picked up pajamas next to Austin's bed, she scanned his nightstand for half-filled glasses of water he liked to place there at bedtime.

She froze when she came face-to-face with Mason.

Her knees gave out and she collapsed of the floor, her gaze never leaving the picture of Austin's father. She hadn't seen that picture in years.

She picked it up and noticed a little piece of paper stuck in the edge. *I love you. Always.*

The words blurred, and her head went fuzzy.

"Mom, can I take—" Austin ran into the room and stopped five feet from her. "Mom…are you…I'm sorry."

She sucked in a breath and got her circulation moving again. She'd been holding her breath that entire time. She dropped her hands and the picture into her lap. "Full sentences, please."

"Are you mad at me for putting my Dad's picture back out?" Her son's frightened eyes darted between her face and the picture.

Elizabeth's heart melted. "No. Not at all. Why would you think I'd be mad?" She'd shown her son that official picture of Mason when he'd been promoted to captain since the day the boy was born.

He hunched his shoulders and looked away.

"Austin, look at me." What the hell was up? Come to think of it, she hadn't seen this picture in years.

"I'm not mad at all." She lifted the picture and looked at her handsome husband, her heart filling with joy that Austin wanted to see it before he went to sleep. Returning her gaze to her son, she asked, "What's wrong?" Maybe he was missing his connection with a father figure and needed the picture again.

He shifted from foot to foot.

"Come here." She patted the floor beside her. He shuffled his feet and plopped down next to her. "I haven't seen this picture in years. Where's it been?"

"Under my bed. Here." He pointed to the space between the mattress and box springs.

"Why did you put it there?" She thought that was a strange place to keep it.

Austin sniffed and looked away.

"No, you don't, young man." She wouldn't allow him to ignore her. "You tell me right now about this picture." She forced his face back around,

"Robert the jerk is gone so now I can have it again." Tears started to roll down his face.

She considered each of his words. "What do you mean, you can have it again?"

The tears flowed. "Robert, I hated him." Gasp. "I'm glad he's dead." His shoulders shook as he cried and huffed in breaths.

Elizabeth pulled her son into her lap and leaned he back against his bed. "I know you two didn't get along, but yes, he's now gone. Now, catch your breath and tell me about this picture of your dad."

It took a few minutes, but Austin gained control. "We were fighting, and Robert chased me into my room."

Oh, shit. Had Robert hit Austin? He hadn't better have ever laid a hand on her son. It took every ounce of patience for her to encourage him to continue.

"He said he was now my father, and my dad was dead." Austin grabbed the picture from the floor and pressed it against his chest. "He told me I was too old for keeping Dad's picture around and that I needed to realize that he was my new Dad. He said he'd take the picture away, so I hid it where he wouldn't find it."

He hiccupped, and she gave him a minute to gain his composure. "Is that all of it?"

She wasn't surprised when he shook his head.

"I said my dad was a hero and he was nothing but some loser that made you pregnant." The tears started again, and Elizabeth cringed at her son's perception of what had happened.

Yes, she'd gotten pregnant soon after they were married but she'd wanted more children. They hadn't told Austin until she started to show. Since he'd been her whole life until she'd married Robert, she'd been worried how he'd take a new father and a new baby. Chalk that up as another motherhood fail. She was already disgusted with herself about Austin's and Robert's failure to build a relationship, but she had no idea how bad it was for her son. If Robert wasn't already dead, she'd kill him.

She pulled her son into her arms, the picture of Mason between them. "I'm so sorry, Austin. You should have told me."

His whole body shook. "Robert said if I told you, then I really was a baby who had to run to his mommy to deal with his problems. That I needed to grow up and be a good big brother to Liza."

She hugged her boy so tight she was afraid she'd break the picture. "You are the best big brother any little girl could ask for." He was such a good kid. How did she ever get so lucky?

They sat like that for a long time, just holding each other. She wondered if Austin had fallen asleep.

"Mommy, Mommy, I gots my toys all packed." At Liza's announcement, both Elizabeth and Austin looked up. She was dragging two carryon bags behind her.

Austin slid off her lap and the slip of paper floated out.

Liza's eyes grew huge.

Elizabeth lifted it when the paper landed on the rug. "Where did you get this?" She knew, of course, but had Austin gone through her room?

He and Liza exchanged a guilty look.

"From the pretty box, Mommy." So, it had been Liza who had searched her room. The girl darted out the door and was back in seconds, Elizabeth's most precious memories in her hands.

"See. The box is so pretty." Liza opened the lid. "I can't read so I brung them to Austin. He's a good reader. I made him keep that one because his daddy loved him."

Elizabeth's heart broke wide open. What her daughter didn't say screamed through the silence. Her father didn't love her.

Austin popped to his feet and put his arm around his little sister. With the eyes of an adult, he bent so they were face to face. "I love you, Liza, Always."

"I know." She smiled as though it was a given. "Mommy loves me, too."

When the doorbell rang, Elizabeth froze. She had no idea who would come to her house.

Matthew stuck his head into the bedroom. "I'll get the door. Grab the children and take them to the master bathroom."

She glanced at the gun in his right hand.

"Get yours on the way in. Whoever is out there will have to get through me to get to you. I want you prepared."

The doorbell rang again.

She jumped up and grabbed the children's hands. As they made their way through the living room, Matthew was already standing at the door.

Gun in hand, the children waiting in the bathroom,

Elizabeth tiptoed across the master bedroom to listen at the cracked door. Matthew was talking to another man. She couldn't understand their words, but the tone was serious yet not unfriendly.

"Have a seat in the living room while I get Elizabeth and the children." Matthew must've been on the move because his voice grew louder.

She slipped into the bathroom and took each child by the hand. They were ready to come out when Matthew knocked on the door.

"Come on out and meet Zeke Gates."

CHAPTER SIXTEEN

"Do you ride?" Matt asked Zeke as they sat adjacent to one another at Lizzie's dining room table.

The younger man smiled. "Raised on a ranch about the size of that one." He pointed to the computer screen where Matt had pulled up a satellite photo of the Sinclair ranch.

"Good. Ask Kenneth Sinclair for good strong riding horse. They have plenty." Matt pointed to a treed section about a half mile from the main house. "A good sniper could make a shot from here. There's access to these woods from this old logging trail. It's only about a four-mile hike. Be sure to check out this area over here, too. You can't tell from this aerial map, but the land rises enough to hide a body. Again, any good sniper could make the shot from a prone position."

Matt stopped and stared at the map, rubbing his scalp, hoping the low-grade headache would go away. How did he know those things he'd just pointed out to Zeke? In his mind he saw them clearly as though he'd ridden the area on horseback and walked the fields in farm boots. Yet, he knew that Matthew St. Clare had never been to the Sinclair farm. In all his research on Mason Sinclair, he couldn't have learned the sniper hides he just pointed out to the Marine captain. What the fuck was going on?

"I'll take good care of your kids," Zeke promised.

"They're not my children." Matt smiled and added, "Yet." He'd never really fought his attraction to Lizzie, and somehow over the past few months, the children had crawled under his skin and into his heart. He felt this desperate need to protect them all. Someone was after their mother, and he doubted they cared about taking out collateral damage at the same time. A shiver of dread ran through his whole body. He was doing everything he could to protect the children that someday he may…no hoped…to call his own.

Kids. He thought he'd never wanted them, until he met Liza and Austin. They had brought more joy to his heart than he'd ever thought possible. Purely by their association with him, they were now targets. Fuck. But no. They were already targets and it had nothing to do with him. But he would protect them at all cost. And their mother. The three of them meant more to him than his own life.

Was it possible to fall in love in just a few months? Yes, he admitted to himself, and he loved them all.

"We're getting there," Lizzie promised, smiling as she walked by with another armful of laundry. "That boy. I swear he'd wear the same jeans every day for a month." She disappeared into the laundry room.

Damn. He wasn't sure which view of her was better, her pretty face with those big silver-gray eyes or her backside. He loved the way her jeans molded to her perfectly sculpted ass. He couldn't wait to rub his big hands over it as she slid down on his cock.

Fuck. Now he was hard. Good thing he was sitting at the table, he'd have time to talk his erection down before he had to stand and embarrass himself. There was just something about that woman that made his dick stand at attention. All it took was her sweet smile, the scent of her as he entered her home, the thought of her as he was alone in his bed. Soon, they'd share the same bed. They both knew it was an inevitability. Hopefully, within the next twenty-four hours. But he had to get the children safe first. He returned his attention back to the computer screen and briefing Zeke on possible points of threat.

In the small hours of the morning, Liza held his hand and her mother's as they walked toward the security area in the nearly empty airport. Matthew noticed Zeke doing the same thing as he did, scanning constantly, noting every door and every person. Thankfully, there were very few people on the redeye flight to Dallas. The head flight attendant had pulled him aside to check his ID. She was much more concerned about a possible terrorist on board, but he had assured her that his office had personally vetted everyone on the flight. Most were businessmen who rarely traveled outside the United States.

Four war-hardened men were part of the Delta team headed back to Kaleen, Texas. Matt had badged them in the waiting area and identified himself. He explained the threat to Elizabeth and the children. The Army lieutenant now walked in front of them with one other man while the other two brought up the rear. They were as secure as they could be in such a public facility.

While they waited at baggage claim, the Delta officer approached Matt. "Sir, we're going to accompany your family to their vehicle. I know you have to hurry to catch your flight home." He glanced to where the conveyor belts started to move. "As soon as we get our bags, we'll be armed." He grinned. "We don't have quite the pull you do with the airlines."

Matt smacked the younger man on the shoulder. "I'll be sure to tell General Lyon how much I appreciated your help."

He dug out his wallet for one of his official business cards that declared him the deputy director of SAD. After writing his personal cell phone number on the card, he handed it to the lieutenant then watched his eyes go wide. Matt grinned. "Let me know if you're ever interested in joining the real bad boys of the world."

"Yes, sir." The first bags started dropping on the belt. "I'd appreciate a good word with the general." The demoralized lieutenant glanced over at his men and sighed. "Our last mission…we didn't get him."

Disappointment filled Matt as the memory of missing Nassar al-Jamil back in Syria ten years ago filled his thoughts. He was positive it was a memory this time. There was no way for it to be anything else. He held out his hand. "I know exactly how you feel." They shook, then both stepped forward to grab bags as they passed by on the carousel.

"Grandpa Dean. Grandma Kate." Liza's unmistakable glee came through every word. "We're going to your house and I'm so excited 'cause I get to stay too."

Matt turned and watched the little girl dash toward his parents.

Yes. They were his parents.

The realization almost knocked him to his knees. He leaned on the suitcase he'd just set down.

Mom. Dad. They seemed to have aged decades.

His love for them returned, first as a trickle, then like a flash flood. He had to fight the searing pain in his head so the floodgates would remain open. Scenes of riding a paint mare, racing his brothers across a field, playing baseball in his high school uniform, his bedroom, prom, Christmas, the heartache of leaving his parents mixed with the excitement of attending West Point, Thanksgiving with a table filled with family, snow covered buildings a century-old at the U.S. Military Academy. Images rushing by like separate frames of a movie based on Mason Sinclair as a youth.

Matt hadn't realized he closed his eyes until he opened them.

He fought the urge to run to his parents, throw his arms around them both, feeling the warmth of their love pour into him.

Then he caught his reflection in the large windows behind them.

Realization smacked him in the face.

They didn't know this man. He was now Matthew St. Clare. Except for his eyes, which were a replica of his father's, he looked nothing like their son.

Elizabeth approached the older couple with a broad smile. "I can't thank you enough for taking care of both children for me."

In that moment, Matt realized he couldn't reveal himself to his parents. He first had to convince Lizzie. If he couldn't prove to her what he was just then comprehending, there was no hope of anyone else understanding. Besides, he felt sure she was falling in love with Matthew St. Clare.

She glanced over her shoulder at Matt and motioned for him to join her.

His feet automatically took him to her side.

"We hope to get the situation resolved quickly, so I can come to Texas and reclaim my children." Elizabeth pulled both her kids into her arms and kissed the tops of their heads. "You two be good for Grandpa Dean and Grandma Katherine," she said in a shaky voice. Tears started to well in her eyes, but she blinked them back.

Matthew couldn't do anything but stare at his parents. The lines in their sun-abused faces had grown deeper and multiplied, their bodies had grown a little thicker, their eyes more hazy. He had missed so much in their lives.

Someone had stolen that time from him. He glanced from his parents to Lizzie and her family. Some fucking son of a bitch had robbed them all of ten years of everyday life, love, tears and joy, none of which they would ever get back. He vowed in that moment that he would tell Lizzie as soon as they returned to Virginia.

As everyone hugged, there was no way Matt could miss the love his parents had for Liza, Austin, and Elizabeth. At least that was one thing to be thankful for, they had gotten to know his son.

He glanced at the boy with curly dark brown hair and the same eyes he looked at in the mirror every morning. The same eyes as his father's. The boy he had gotten to know and love was his son.

Matthew couldn't breathe. He had a child. He and Lizzie had created a baby. But Austin was no infant. At nine years old he had been influenced by other men, a job he should have been doing. Matt hoped that Dean Sinclair had taught Austin many of life's lessons the way Mason had learned them. His father was a good man. He'd raised good sons, and a hard-working daughter.

Lizzie touched his arm pulling him back to the present. "This is a friend of mine, Matthew St. Clare." She glanced at him and gave him a small smile. "He's helping me sort out my situation."

His father held out his hand as though to a stranger. The truth in the gesture shot a knife blade of pain through Matt's heart. No, it was Mason's heart that was hurting. Separating the two was becoming more difficult with every second.

When their hands connected his father's gaze flew to his and held for a long minute. "You look familiar, son. Have we met before?"

Matthew wanted to jerk the man into his arms and hug him tight. He was sure his father did not refer to him as his son, because the man had always called every male a few decades younger, son. He purposely ignored the question. "Thank you for taking care of the children." Diverting the attention away from himself, he signaled to Zeke. "Sir, I'd like you to meet Zeke Gates. He'll be the children's personal security. I'd appreciate it if you gave him free range of the ranch. I've arranged to enhance the security system on the house and the perimeter. Zeke will be overseeing that installation."

Turning his attention to Zeke, Matt gave him some final instructions. "The items we ordered this afternoon should be delivered within a few days. You have my numbers. Don't hesitate to call."

"I've got this," Zeke reassured him. In a quiet voice so only he could hear, he added, "Get that fucker, then come get your kids." He looked at his watch. "You two have a plane to catch. Better get going." As though a silent gong had struck indicating their time together had come to an end, Elizabeth gave the Sinclair's one more hug goodbye, then picked up Liza. Austin turned and ran to Matt, throwing his arms out. He caught his son and held him tight for the first time.

The little boy sweat that had become so familiar, filled his senses. His son was solid, so much like his own build at that age. Matt ran his hand through the soft dark curls and held the boy's head to his chest. He wanted to remember everything about this moment, not just because it was the first, but because it was the first of many to come. He looked at the reflection in the window and silently cursed the man who had stolen moments like this from him for the past decade. He wasn't there to see his child be born, nor hold him as an infant. He hadn't seen Austin take his first steps or heard his first word.

Matt fought off the anger that threatened to fill his heart and savored the goodness of the moment.

"Take good care of my mom," the child said in a choked voice. "I promise to practice baseball every day I can so I'm real good by the time we get back home."

A fist grabbed Matt's heart and his throat thickened. "You do everything Zeke tells you to do. He's there to keep you safe. You still have the card I gave you, right? You can call me anytime day or night."

Austin patted his pocket. "I got it right here." He gave Matt one last hug then crawled out of his embrace. He sprinted to his mother and hugged her around the waist since she was still holding Liza. The little girl looked up and waved at him. She kissed her hand and waved it toward him, blowing him a kiss. Christ, he loved that little girl. As soon as he and Elizabeth were married, he was going to adopt her.

Marry Elizabeth. He chuckled.

They were already married.

CHAPTER SEVENTEEN

It was nearly eleven o'clock in the morning by the time Matthew and Elizabeth dragged their extremely tired bodies into her home. Except for a few tears from Liza, and a few her mother had held back, their goodbyes had been brief. He and Lizzie had just made it back to the boarding gate when he received a text from the Army Lieutenant with a photograph of taillights. *Headed home.* He quickly responded with: *Thanks. Offer stands.*

Maybe someday was the reply.

What Matt needed now was the sleep that had evaded him on the crowded plane ride home. Remaining vigilant wasn't a problem. Too many thoughts had occupied his mind during the last several hours. Lizzie had to learn the truth first. If he couldn't convince her of his identity, and that he'd been...he wasn't even sure what to call it. Brainwashed? Reprogrammed? Deceived to the point he thought he was a completely different person? Had his memory erased?

The name for the procedure wasn't nearly as important as the reason why it had happened. On that point, he had no clue. He was fairly certain that the CIA had messed with his brain. They wanted him to forget everything associated with Mason Sinclair and his previous life.

Perusing his psychological files yesterday morning had proven enlightening. He discovered that he underwent intensive psychological debriefing ten years ago, after recovering from several surgeries he'd needed to correct the damage from his accident. There was never an actual mention of a car, just the word *accident*. An accident that took place the same day Mason Sinclair had died in an explosion in a small village in Syria.

He still didn't remember anything about the mission, no matter how hard he tried. Much of his memory was coming back in disjointed snippets. As he'd held Elizabeth while she slept on the plane, their single honeymoon night had come back to him.

Getting married was a last-minute decision. After three days of hard training nearly round-the-clock, they'd made a mad dash to the Cumberland County Courthouse, the last ones in the door before they were closed for the day. The clerk issued them the marriage license and Mason had just paid the sixty-dollar fee when a man in blue jeans, a pressed blue button-down shirt, and cowboy boots strode to the counter and dropped off a stack of papers. Mason was asking the clerk if there was anyone around who could marry them right then. The woman glanced up at the retreating man's back.

Before she could say a word, the man in his mid-fifties spun around. "After the day I've had, I need something good in my life." He stared at the two of them. Mason remembered his heart beating so fast with anticipation. "Why are you two in such an all-fire hurry to get married?"

Mason had stepped forward and extended his hand. "Sir, I'm Captain Mason Sinclair, and this is my fiancé Lieutenant Elizabeth Kamp. There's a damn good chance we're both being deployed in the next couple days. We want to make it official before we get shipped out."

The older gentleman took his hand in a surprisingly firm shake. "Sounds like a damn good reason. I'm Judge Brian O'Malley. How fast you want this ceremony?"

"Fast," Elizabeth said as she held out her hand to shake. "We're expected back on base for supper."

The red-haired man with silver-tipped temples burst out laughing. "Well, then let's get this over with. Elizabeth, do you take Mason to be your husband?"

She was grinning ear to ear. "Yes, sir."

"Mason, do you take Elizabeth to be your wife?"

"Yes, sir. I do." With those words, followed by signatures from the judge and the two clerks behind the counter, Lizzie became his wife.

After a working dinner with their team, Mason had taken his new wife to a moderately priced hotel just outside the main gate of Fort Bragg. Fully dressed, they had collapsed on the bed, in each other's arms...and promptly fell asleep. Sometime in the middle of the night, they had awakened, gently stripped off each other's clothes, and made slow passionate love before falling asleep again. Just before dawn, both their cell phones had gone off. Three hours later they were wheels up and on the way to Syria.

That was all Matt could remember. He didn't even remember the plane landing.

There had been some unusual indications in his medical records that included a transfer from Germany to Walter Reed National Military Medical Center. It was common knowledge that anyone hurt in the Middle East went to Germany first, but Matthew's car accident supposedly happened on the D.C. Beltway.

After hours of intensive research the previous day, he'd ended up with more questions than answers. At the moment though, his brain was too tired to connect the jigsaw pieces, especially when so many were still missing.

Lizzie set her purse on the table next to the door where it usually sat waiting for its next trip. When he closed the door behind him, she turned and set the alarm. She looked relatively refreshed, especially given the last twenty-four hours. She'd slept nearly three hours on the flight home, nestled in his arms.

She turned from the keypad and wreathed her arms around his neck. "There are no children in this house." She gave him a salacious smile. "We can be adults anywhere we want."

Although she was offering herself to him, Matthew wasn't comfortable with her continuing to stay there. Whoever was after her must have followed them from her house to the mall. He was positive no one followed them to the airport last night, but her staying at home made her an even more visible target.

"Tempting offer. The problem is, you're not safe here. I want you to come and stay with me. My house has a state-of-the-art surveillance system including the entire perimeter. Lizzie, I need you to pack a bag." When she started to protest, he kissed her long and slow and deep. Holding her felt so right. It always had. Now, he had to make sure she was in his future.

He broke the kiss, twisted her around, and pointed her toward the bedroom. "Go pack enough clothes for at least a week. If it takes any longer than that, you can come back and get more." He swatted her beautifully rounded ass.

"You're going to pay for that Matthew St. Clare." Given the smile on her face, he was looking forward to the punishment.

"You don't need to bring anything to sleep in," he called just before she disappeared into the master bedroom.

"Promises, promises," she hollered back.

Matt glanced around to see if there was anything he needed to do to close down the house for a few days. It was a little bit warm inside, but he thought she might keep the temperature higher so that the air conditioning didn't kick on as often, saving on utility bills. Hopefully soon she wouldn't have to worry about that anymore. Once he got her to his house, she wasn't going to leave.

On his next breath, he smelled the garbage. He could take it to the outside can for her while she packed. He'd been the one to cook breakfast yesterday morning. It almost smelled like the eggshells were rotting.

Five minutes later, the ugly task completed and fresh bags in both the trash and recycling cans, he walked through the entire house one more time checking all the doors and windows, assuring himself the home was locked tight.

When Elizabeth emerged from her bedroom rolling two bags behind her, her smile was a little nervous, but her eyes were excited. "I'll just put these in my car and follow you over."

"No. I'd rather your neighbors believe you're home. Let's leave your car in the garage for now and take mine." Matthew was afraid if someone thought Elizabeth was elsewhere, they would go looking for her. Eventually, they would connect his presence at the mall with her. Although he was hard to find, he knew how persistent his men were in tracking a target. No doubt whomever was after Elizabeth was equally as skilled.

Twenty minutes later, he drove up the long driveway to his house.

"Nice place," she commented.

He glanced up and tried to see his home through her eyes. It was rather big for just him. The two-story brick colonial had been the right price when he moved back to CIA headquarters. What he had liked about it was that it sat on a full acre surrounded by a comfortable buffer of trees. He didn't care for neighbors too close. He only saw his during the winter when the deciduous trees lost their leaves, but he had eyes everywhere on his property. His woods were filled with state-of-the-art security equipment. He knew everything that happened within the boundaries of his land, including how often the squirrels fucked. Lizzie would be in the safest house possible.

Now, if he could get her into his bed, she'd be even safer.

He easily carried her bags from the garage, through the kitchen and set them down at the bottom of the steps. "I have four bedrooms, but one I've converted into a home gym, so you have your choice of either staying in a guestroom or with me." To influence her choice, he leaned forward and kissed her. It started out tender, but she grabbed his head and pulled him even closer while opening her mouth to him.

"Any questions as to my choice?" She glanced around at the formal living room and formal dining room, then through the eat-in kitchen area to the large family room. "Master bedroom upstairs?"

"Is there anything you need in the bags in the next ten minutes?"

She shook her head as though she couldn't speak.

He snaked an arm around her shoulder and under her knees and carried her up the wide staircase directly to the master suite.

"I've pictured you in my bed so many times. I can't believe you're really here." He let her feet fall to the floor, her body sliding over his. There was no way she could miss his erection. Part of him wanted to take it slow, but he was afraid he couldn't. This was Lizzie. Although he hadn't been naked with her in his bed in over ten years, he knew that in her mind, she was about to have sex with Matthew St. Clare.

He wanted to have this time with her making love with the man he was now. In so many ways, Mason Sinclair was dead. He was a different man now. Obviously, Lizzie liked him the way he was. She had loved him before. She could learn to love him again.

When the time was right, he would tell her who he was in the past, what little bit of it he could remember. Thankfully, more memories returned every day. He needed to concentrate on today and build on that new foundation.

"I want you so much, but I'm afraid this first time I'm not going to be able to love you the way I want to. You deserve tenderness as I worship every inch of your body." The last ten years of Matthew's life had been a lie, and he didn't want to lie anymore, especially to his Lizzie. He needed her to know exactly how he felt.

She cupped his face and looked deep into his eyes. "Matthew, at our age we know what we want from sex. I wouldn't be standing here if I didn't want you inside me, giving me the orgasms I believe you can. Neither of us is new to sex, although I admit I haven't been intimate with a man in nearly a year."

This revelation shocked Matthew. "But your husband's only been—"

She looked away for a second before returning her gaze to his. "Robert and I had difficulties in our marriage that increased every year." She shrugged. "I was afraid after Liza was born that he just didn't find me"—she swallowed hard —"appealing anymore." She rolled her lips in as though biting back the words. "I was right." Her voice broke on those three little words. So did his heart.

Matthew couldn't allow her to think of herself as anything but the beautiful, sexy woman she was. "I was attracted to you the very first time I ever saw you and that was months before we actually met. You walked away from Gabriel toward the front door at headquarters in that sexy suit that cupped that beautiful ass of yours." He slid his hands and cupped both butt cheeks, pressing her against his body so she could feel his hard-as-steel cock. "Your husband was a fucking idiot."

He kissed her then, trying to convey just how much he wanted her. They tilted their heads in opposite directions, so they could both go deeper. He had never been so in sync with a woman as Matthew St. Clare. He now understood why. No one could compare to his Lizzie, and no woman ever would. She had always been the only woman for him. Somewhere deep inside him, he had recognized her, knew she was his and was supposed to be forever. He had never stopped loving her.

His hands dropped to the breasts he hadn't touched in a decade. They were fuller, rounder, heavier than he remembered. That probably came with having children. He couldn't wait to take them in his mouth and savor their new size.

He felt the heat of Lizzie's hands on his chest as she started to unbutton his dress shirt. She was fumbling. He hadn't expected her nervousness. He cupped both his hands around hers. "We can take this slow."

Sharp gray eyes met his. "Matthew, I don't want slow. I want this first time to be hard and fast." She took his hand and shoved it down her pants, pressing his fingers into her folds which were drenched with need. "I want you to make me come so hard and so fast." She pressed his hand down she rocked her hips against his fingers. He automatically curled them searching for her clitoris.

Her head fell back as she moaned when he found the hard button of nerves.

Victory. Her ecstasy was literally in his hand. She wanted him as much as he wanted her.

"I don't want to deny you anything, but I want you in my bed, especially the first time." He kissed her briefly. "Promise me, though, next time you will let me remove every stitch of your clothing, but right now I want you to take your clothes off." He slowly removed his hand caressing her clit one more time. He stuck his wet fingers into his mouth and savored the taste of Lizzie for the first time in ten years. His body remembered her, and so did his mind as several memories of tasting her with his tongue rushed back.

She lifted her blouse over her head, and he immediately took her mouth, sharing her own flavor with her. Deftly, he unsnapped her bra. Before it hit the floor, his hands cupped both breasts. They were soft, fuller than he remembered. He massaged them lightly then rolled the nipples between his thumbs and forefingers. She rocked her hips into him as she reached for his belt.

Tearing her lips away from his, she demanded, "Hurry. I'll get my jeans." She stroked him through his khaki slacks, squeezing slightly then rubbing a finger across the tip.

Christ, nothing had ever felt so good as her hand on his cock. If she did it again, it might be over before they got started. He took her hands and put them on her snap and zipper. "Do that again, and you might not get your wish for an hour. I'm not the young man I used to be. Although I can assure you, I'm good for several times in one night, but it takes me a little while to recover."

She pushed down her jeans and left on her white panties, but he could see her dark hair through the nearly transparent lace. His cock throbbed against his zipper. He followed her lead and let his pants drop to the floor, leaving him in boxer briefs, his cock barely restrained behind the pocket.

She stared for a long second before reaching for the edges of her panties.

"No, please. Let me." He kneeled in front of her, smelling

that unique scent that had always been Lizzie. A memory of him in that same position on the night they'd gotten engaged pushed its way through. He fought back the headache that threatened at his temples and concentrated on how happy they both were that night. They'd made love slowly, tenderly, taking their time bringing each other to the edge and over three times before they'd fallen asleep.

Matt hooked his thumbs around the top edge and pulled them down. Running his fingers down her legs the way she had liked before. When her calves quivered, he knew he was successful. "Step out and spread your legs."

She did as ordered.

He leaned in and opened her folds, exposing her elongated, swollen clit. Taking it in his mouth he sucked, rubbing his tongue along the bottom. She'd liked that before, too. He was remembering more and more of the way she preferred to be touched.

Her fingers wove through his hair and dug in when he sucked hard.

"I know you can come more than once. Let yourself go, Lizzie. I've got you." He shoved two fingers into her hot channel, and she cried out her release. His fingers were clenched as her whole body shook.

When her knees gave out, she dropped onto his lap and threw her arms around his neck resting her head on his shoulder. He stayed with her, pumping his fingers in and out and rubbing her clit with his thumb until she was breathing smoothly. He extracted his fingers and shoved them in his mouth. He had to taste her release.

The heat of her center was right up against his cock, separated only by his boxer briefs. He started running batting scores through his head to take his mind off the erection that wanted to move into her.

They sat on the floor like that for several minutes before

Lizzie finally lifted her head. She gave him a sated smile. "I haven't had an orgasm like that in years." She giggled. "I want to say thank you." She rocked forward rubbing her open folds against his underwear. "I think we need to take care of this now."

She started to stand, and he followed her up, lifting her onto his bed. He shucked off his boxer briefs before lying on top of her, using his knees to spread hers until she was completely open to him. "Lizzie, please tell me you're on the pill or some other means of birth control. I had my five-year physical almost six months ago, and I haven't been with anyone since then." He smiled down at her. "That was the first day I saw you, and the last day I even looked at another woman. Somehow, I knew we'd end up like this. If at all possible, I don't want anything between us when we make love."

She looked hesitant, so he leaned over to the nightstand and opened the drawer. He'd placed a new box of condoms there, hoping that one day Lizzie would be in his bed, once again. As he reached for a packet, her hand stopped him.

Their gazes locked and neither said anything for several heartbeats. Finally, she spoke. "Matthew, I trust you. Yes, I'm on the pill. This may sound terrible, but I didn't want to get pregnant again with Robert. I guess I'd known for a long time he and I—"

Matthew leaned down and kissed her. He didn't want to hear anything about that man or think about him with Lizzie. The rational part of him was overjoyed that her marriage wasn't a happy one. He would make it his life's mission to keep a smile on her face, give her anything she wanted, be the man she needed.

She broke away from him for moment. "I want you inside me. Now!"

As he slid into the woman he had always loved, it was like

becoming whole. The part of him that had been missing was suddenly reconnected. He was joining his soul to hers. As he pumped in and out, her inner walls clamping him tight, he could only hope that she would open up her heart to him once again.

"I know you're close, sweetheart. What can I do to get you there?" He wanted them to both come at the same time. He knew she could do it.

"Suck my breasts." She raised her hips up to meet his thrusts, forcing him as deep as possible. Heaven couldn't be this sweet.

Bending his head, he took a nipple into his mouth and sucked hard. He rolled his hips so his pubic bone ground against her clitoris. Her nipples hardened and her hips rose off the bed. She gasped. He moved to the other nipple and repeated the process. This time she wrapped her strong legs around his waist and hooked her ankles, changing their angle. Matthew didn't think he'd ever been so deep in a woman before. She was so tight and felt beyond good, better than great. He licked the first nipple then bit lightly.

Elizabeth screamed as she bucked them both. Satisfied she was coming, he let loose and fell over the edge with her. He wanted to collapse on top of her, but rolled to one side taking her with him while staying connected.

He held her naked body to his, never wanting to let go.

CHAPTER EIGHTEEN

Elizabeth awoke when she felt something warm and wet between her legs. Matthew's hot breath heated her entire pelvic area but something a little abrasive, yet wonderful, brushed up and down her folds. She took a deep breath bringing herself back from the ecstasy he'd shown her. Damn, the man was good. Mason had been the only man to make her reach an orgasm while he was inside her and that had happened rarely. Matthew had achieved that goal, and then some. He seemed to know exactly what to do with her body and what she liked. He'd been able to bring her to the peak within minutes.

She looked down at Matthew's white hair, so soft and slightly wavy, she couldn't resist but to thread her fingers through it.

He looked up at her and smiled. "You're awake."

Her smile matched his. "Yes, I am. What are you doing down there? I'm not complaining, just curious."

He held up a washcloth. "We were both sticky. One of the side effects of riding bareback."

She wondered how he knew that. How many women had

he brought to this very bed? How many other women had he convinced they didn't need a condom?

He slid up the bed next to her, covering them both with the warm blankets. He ran a finger over her brow. "Wipe that look off your face. You are my first for so many things. No other woman has ever been in this bed."

Well, hell. Could he read her mind?

He continued, "The only other woman I've been inside of without a condom was my wife and that was just over ten years ago."

A pang of sorrow hit her hard. She rolled onto her side and ran her fingertips over his forehead, down his cheeks to his square jaw. It was like touching the face of an angel. He was so beautiful in a very masculine way. "I'm sorry. Are you divorced or widowed?"

She watched emotions flit across his face before he smiled. "Neither."

She pushed back away from him. "You're still married?"

He pulled her back to him, aligning their bodies chest to chest, hip to hip. "Lizzie, did you ever wonder why we had an instant connection?"

She took a few minutes to think about it. She had felt something when they'd met. That had never happened to her before. "Why? Do you believe in reincarnation? Do you think we were together in a previous life?"

Matt chuckled. "That might be closer to the truth than you would believe."

Lizzie stared at him, not sure how to take his statement.

Matthew let out a heavy slow sigh. "Did Mason have a birthmark?"

Her eyes went wide. How could he have known that? Well, it might've been in his record somewhere as an identifying mark. At least he didn't have any tattoos. "Yes. On the inside of his right hip."

"A zigzag, shaped something like an M connected to a K." For the first time, Matthew looked worried. He lowered the sheet to expose his right hip.

Lizzie stared at the dark brown jagged line. It couldn't be. No two people could have such a unique birthmark. Maybe it was a scar that looked like Mason's birthmark. What kind of game was this man playing. Who had she just slept with? She tore her gaze from the mark on his body and met his eyes. She needed a closer look, so she crawled over to examine it closely.

It was a birthmark. Exactly the same as Mason had.

"The first time you saw my birthmark, you told me you had thought it was a tattoo. You were going to ask me whose initials were MK."

Oh my God. That's exactly what happened. She glanced up at him then returned her gaze to the mark he'd had since birth.

"Lizzie, you have kissed that birthmark. You have licked it, traced it with the tip of your tongue. It has fascinated you since the first day you ever saw it, the first time we made love on your bunk at Fort Campbell."

No. No one but Mason could know those things.

She looked up at him then and held his eyes prisoner. Yes, they were the correct color, exactly like her son's. But the face. Although he was the most handsome man she had ever known in her life, that was not Mason's face. She glanced back at the birthmark then into eyes that had gone liquid gold with passion moments ago, just like they had ten years ago.

No. Mason is dead. He died years ago. She'd moved on. It was so difficult, but she had to keep going. She had a baby to think about, care for, and consider as she made every decision by herself. Teagan had been there when she'd had Austin because his father was dead. She got out of the Army because she didn't want to go away to war and leave her son behind. If anything had happened to her, her beautiful little boy would be parentless. She'd made arrangements, should the worst possible happen, that Teagan would raise him like her own. But Elizabeth had moved on because Mason was dead. She had married Robert and had her precious daughter.

"No! You can't be Mason. He's dead." She started to crawl out of bed, but he grabbed her. She was trapped, not just in his arms, but in his house. He had convinced her not to bring her car. Could she get out of the house? Maybe. But where would she go? She didn't see any neighbors nearby. She had to think her way out of this situation. "What kind of sick joke are you trying to play here, Matthew?"

Calmly he answered, "It's no joke, Lizzie. Do you remember the cowboy judge who married us?"

Of course she did. "You could've looked up our marriage license then did a Google search on the judge. Perhaps somewhere it referred to his boots and jeans."

"He asked us how fast we wanted the wedding. You said fast before I could even open my mouth."

"That's exactly what happened." But Elizabeth still wasn't convinced. Only Mason would know the answer to her next question. "What happened when we got to the hotel room?"

He chuckled. "We were both so fucking tired we collapsed onto the bed with our clothes on." He raised one eyebrow. "Convinced yet?"

No. Yes.

In a flash she was on top of him, beating his chest with her fists. "Where the hell have you been? I needed you. Our son needed you. Where the fuck did you go?" Then she laid her palms on his cheeks. "And why did you change your face? I loved you just the way you were."

Tears were running in streams down her cheeks. He brushed them away with his thumbs, just like he used to.

"I swear to God, Lizzie, I don't know." He leaned in and kissed her. "I was hoping you had the answers."

Now she was totally confused. "How? Why?" She was still having a very difficult time wrapping her mind around the fact that the man in this bed was her dead husband.

"No! Mason is dead. I buried him ten years ago," she insisted.

"No, you buried an empty box ten years ago. The reason the SEAL team didn't find any remnants of Mason Sinclair was because there were none to find." He glanced away. "That part of my memory still hasn't returned." He rubbed his temples. "I don't remember anything at all after we went wheels up toward Syria."

It dawned on her. "The headaches. That happens every time a memory comes back?" She thought about the many times that he had rubbed his head next to his eyes. The tears began to flow again.

"You forgot all about me." Her heart broke all over again. She had cried for months after losing Mason.

He kissed her on top of the head. "I'm not sure I forgot about you or if someone suppressed that part of my memory."

Her head shot up so she could look into his eyes. "Someone? You were brainwashed?"

"I have no idea. According to my psychological records, I spent several months in debriefing after an accident." He made air quotes around the last word. "That accident took place the same day as the explosion where Mason was supposedly killed."

"You made it out of the munitions dump? How? Where did you go?" All she had was questions for him.

Matthew shrugged. Or was he Mason? "I have no idea. My memory has been coming back in flashes, sometimes dreams, all too often nightmares. I never know when a memory will push through." He then smiled at her. "The best memories I have are of you. I now have dozens of them. As I tasted you an hour ago, my brain was flooded with the many times I licked you, sucked your clit, and fingered you until you fell apart in my arms. You were always the one thing I remembered. It wasn't until I saw you leaving headquarters that day, I knew Elizabeth Kamp was the woman I had been dreaming about for years."

Now she was mad. Angry beyond belief. She laid her hands on his cheeks. "Someone stole all those years from us." She looked into eyes the color of her son's. "Do you realize that Austin is your son? Our son. Someone cheated us out of our life together, but worse, they cheated Austin out of his father. Who the fuck did this to you? To us."

His grin was sarcastic. "Who do you think? Who do we work for? Who can be the biggest bastards on this planet? They believe they own us twenty-four-seven."

"What? The CIA did this to us?" She found that hard to believe. "Why?"

"I don't know. At this point, I can't trust any of my memories." He leaned up and kissed her.

She suddenly remembered how many times they had talked for hours in bed, holding each other, kissing, and recuperating before they made love again. She snuggled into him, just like she had done so many years before.

"Okay, let's think about this logically. Let's start at the beginning. Mason was supposedly killed in the explosion in Syria." She leaned up and kissed him because she could. She was so thankful that he was alive and hers once again. "By the way, when did you realize that you were both Mason and Matthew?"

He chuckled. "Just a few hours ago actually. When I saw my mom and dad in Dallas. At that moment I was positive. Up until then, I thought my parents were dead and that I had been raised on a desolate farm in Wyoming. They had gone so far as to convince me that I had sold that farm which was getting ready to be taken for taxes, and that's how I paid for this house."

"Oh my God. We have to tell your parents, and your brothers, and your sister that you are alive." She pulled up on one elbow and looked down at him. "If you knew back in Dallas, why didn't you say something to your parents then?"

He pulled her down for a kiss. "Because I had to tell you first. I had to make you believe me before I could even try to tell anyone else."

Damn, if that wasn't the sweetest thing anybody had ever said to her. She leaned down and kissed him. "Thank you for that." She hugged him tight against her naked body. "I have missed you so much."

They needed to continue figuring this out before the waterworks turned on again.

"So, you don't remember anything at all about our last mission together?" Elizabeth rolled her head to see him but stayed plastered to his chest.

"I've read what's in the reports, but we both know sometimes those can be fairytales." He spoke the truth. More than once they had stretched the facts in a report.

She scoffed. "And those can be easily changed if you have the right clearance."

"The files said one of the charges went off early, and I was still inside the building. And before you ask, I have no idea what happened. When I woke up, I had a new face and my name was Matthew St. Clare. I've been told my face was smashed in when the airbag didn't release during a car accident on the D.C. Beltway. Until I saw the gravestone at the cemetery, the day I met you, I had never heard of Mason Sinclair."

She thought about that day and several that had followed.

"There was never an investigation into Mason's death was there?"

At least he had the good grace to look sheepish. "Oh, there was an investigation. Mine. But no, the agency was not involved in any way."

"That's why you wanted all the secrecy." She was beginning to understand. He didn't know who to trust, and now, neither did she.

It was his turn to lean in and kiss her. "You always were a smart woman."

"If I'm so damn smart, why haven't we figured this out yet?" Elizabeth's stomach growled. "I'm starved. Do you have anything to eat in this house?"

He pulled her closer and rocked his hips, so she felt his erection poking her. "You were always very good at—"

She smacked him. "I need food. Sustenance. If I remember right, you can cook." Then she remembered the blueberry pancakes he prepared for her and the children. He looked so right, comfortable in that role. "Breakfast was always your specialty." She smiled at him. "Feed me," she demanded, then rolled off the bed. She looked around and remembered her suitcases were sitting at the bottom of the stairs.

He got up from the other side of the bed and padded naked to the highboy dresser. Opening the third drawer, he tossed her one of his T-shirts. She looked around for her underwear, but before she could grab them, he snatched them from the floor.

"You are not going to need these. I want you naked under that T-shirt." His grin was filled with promise. "I haven't christened any of the flat surfaces in this house. I've been waiting for you." He kissed her then slipped on a pair of sleep pants, commando.

Thirty minutes later, they had finished their omelets at

his walnut formal dining room table. The intricate inlay was absolutely gorgeous and coordinated with the side pieces in a masculine style. She glanced into the living room dominated by dark brown leather accented with light brown and red pillows.

"Who decorated your house for you?" When he was Mason, the man wouldn't be able to color coordinate his own clothing, say nothing about an entire house. It was a good thing he was in the Army, and they told him every day which uniform to wear.

He glanced around and didn't look at her. "You really want the answer to that question?"

No, not really. "Yes."

"I dated an interior decorator for about a month." He didn't look happy at the confession.

"Just a month?" Why was she torturing herself this way? He had no idea she even existed back then. Hell. She had gotten married and had created a child with another man. She loved Liza with every ounce of her heart. That little girl was the best thing Robert had ever given her.

The edges of Matthew's mouth twitched. "I needed furniture. She sold furniture. She sold me a lot of furniture. After a few weeks of dating, I realized she was very good at spending my money." He reached over and laid his hand on her bare knee. "She wasn't very good at other things. And since we're on the subject, I need you to know, I dated a lot in the last ten years." He leaned over and kissed her. "But none of them stuck. I think my longest relationship was with my plastic surgeon."

"I'm hoping your plastic surgeon was a woman," she interjected.

"Jessica is definitely a woman. She wanted me for my looks, the face that she had created, not for the man I was." He grinned sardonically. "She's made millions of dollars off my face." He touched the edges where she could see very thin pink scars. "I've seen the before and after pictures hundreds of times. I'm still amazed at what a skillful surgeon she is. Personally, I'm just thankful my eyes weren't damaged."

"I have always loved your eyes," she admitted. "I got to see them every single day since Austin was born. Did you know that I gave him your last name? Your mother was so happy I did that."

He cupped the back of her head and pulled it toward him, kissing her with a ferocity she hadn't yet seen in him. "I love that you did that for me."

He stood and grabbed the dishes, rinsing them before he put them in the dishwasher. He turned on her and, faster than she could imagine, he scooped her up. "The whole time I was eating lunch on that dining room table, all I could think about was eating you."

He laid her on the table, sat in the chair at the end, placing her bare feet on the armrests. Mason had always been playful, but Matthew took sex to a whole new level. He had her writhing within minutes but wouldn't let her come until he was deep inside her. With her back flat on the table, perfect height for him to stand and slide into her, it only took a few flicks of his thumb over her clit before she completely fell apart, taking him with her.

Boneless, they headed toward the stairs. Another nap was definitely needed. As they walked through the living room, Elizabeth admired the view of the backyard. "This is absolutely gorgeous. So private." She could picture Matthew and Austin playing baseball and a swing set for Liza, maybe one of those with an attached fort. She could easily picture herself living there, the life that she and Mason—or would he want to continue to be called Matthew—should have been living the last ten years.

They only made it as far as the couch before they collapsed and had fallen asleep in each other's arms once again.

The next time they woke, it was night. Hungry once again, they had decided to shower before Elizabeth insisted on making them a decent supper. She had never had shower sex before, but she could now check that off her list. She was sure that Matthew's list was longer than hers.

She had slipped into a pair of yoga pants and a long T-shirt, something she often slept in. Matthew had pulled on a pair of jeans and nothing else. They talked as they cooked supper together.

He was seasoning the steaks when he announced, "We need to figure out who is behind your attacks. I can't help but think my memory loss, or reprogramming, has something to do with the current situation. Go back to that day in Syria. Try to remember. Did you see anyone else there? We've already determined that Logan and Micah were up on a hill about half a mile away."

She had just finished painting the asparagus with olive oil and reached for the salt-and-pepper as she picked up the story. "You went in first. That wasn't the way we trained, but you insisted that your Special Forces training was so much better than ours, and you were going to handle the charges in the back of the building. Teagan and I followed you in and took the first several rooms, as we'd practiced a hundred times."

"Who else was on site? When one of our SOG teams goes in, we have a local asset and sometimes the regional handler is there." Matthew flipped the steak and seasoned the other side.

"Well, Gabe was there, of course, but I don't remember any local asset. I'm pretty sure Gabe had the intel on the area. He'd met us at the landing zone and took us directly to the building where the Russian munitions were being stored." Remembering even more, she added, "A SEAL team was chasing Nassar al Jamil and they were about forty miles away. That's why you decided to help us plant the charges, so we could all get out of there faster." She went over and put her arms around his waist. "We were going to go on a honeymoon when we returned stateside. Then we were going to go tell our parents that we got married."

"I'm sorry, but I don't remember any of that." He looked disturbed.

"What do you remember?" she probed.

"Nothing about the mission. It's as though I woke up in pain from the accident…Christ, the pain was unbearable." He rubbed the spot next to his eye and winced. "The next thing I knew, I was in physical therapy and Jessica was putting the moves on me." He gave her a look of innocence. "In my mind, I was unattached and she was beautiful, and…" he trailed off, keeping his back to Lizzie.

Matthew turned and held her. "I didn't know I was married. We were married. I didn't remember until a few hours ago." He shook his head. "I'm fucking this up. What I'm trying to say is that there were a lot of women in the past ten years. Gorgeous, young…"

The last couple hours had been as though they were married, living and acting like they hadn't been separated for the past decade. But they hadn't been together. He'd had ten years of bachelor life. With his movie star looks, she was positive he hadn't lacked for companionship, but she didn't want to think about the younger, beautiful women he'd slept with.

Hell, she'd dated a few men then married Robert. They had both changed so much, how dare she assume that he would want her in his life every day. Robert had tired of her very quickly. Matthew would also. Why would he want to take on a middle-aged woman and her two children? True, one of those children was his, and he would no doubt want to support his son, but she came as a package deal. Not a very good one.

"Whoa," he ran his fingers over the scowl wrinkles on her for head. "I knew I was doing a terrible job explaining away the past decade, but I need you to understand that I didn't know about us. Talk to me."

She pointed toward the beautiful backyard, now black with night, and instantly teared up. "When I saw that gorgeous backyard, I thought what a wonderful place for Austin and Liza to play. I have no idea how you—"

"I love you Elizabeth Kamp. I always have. I loved you as Mason, and I think I have been looking for you for the past ten years. Now that I found you, I'm not letting you go." He glanced out the living room window toward the darkened backyard. "When I bought this house, I didn't even think about children playing out there, but now I see a swing set for Liza and a batter's net in that corner over there for Austin. Maybe a pretty flower garden along the side, so when we sit out on the deck we have beautiful colors to look at." He pulled her into his arms. "Now that you're here, you are never leaving."

"You just said you never planned on children.," she protested. "I have two."

"I never planned on finding you. You've already given me the greatest gift a man could ever want, your love and two of the most wonderful children I've ever met. You have done an awesome job raising them. Will you let me help raise Liza and Austin?" His big hand went to her belly. "And any other children we have, if you want more babies." He then kneeled in front of her. "Elizabeth Kamp, would you please marry me...again?"

The heat from her tears warmed her cheeks. Damn. She

was crying so much these days. What the hell was with that. But this striking man, her personal angel, had just asked her to marry him. She had a good reason to cry.

"I'm not sure we need to get married. You're not dead." She stated the obvious.

"No, he's not. Neither are you, and that's the real problem." The voice came from the direction of the family room. Gabe stepped into the light, a gun in his hand.

Matthew stood up in front of her. She was in such shock to see their friend that she tried to step around the man she loved.

Gabe shook his head as he walked into the living room. "Elizabeth. Elizabeth. Elizabeth. I liked you. I've tried to help you every chance I could. But you fucked this up big time." He then laughed. "Literally. Well, I'm glad you at least had a few good orgasms before you died."

"What the hell are you talking about, Gabe?" Why was he there? Why did he have a gun pointed at them?

"You have my house wired." It was a statement, not a question. Matthew sounded more pissed than surprised.

Gabe smiled. "Audio and video. Every room."

Elizabeth was devastated. Someone had watched them as they had made love on... *Oh my God*. They had done it ...she couldn't stop her eyes as her gaze flew to the dining room table.

Gabe's smile grew bigger. "Elizabeth, if I'd known you were that adventurous, I would've gotten rid of Robert sooner just so I could sample a taste of your wild side."

"You shut the fuck up." Matthew growled. "Don't you talk to my wife that way."

"Thanks for the confirmation Matthew, or should I call you Mason? We weren't sure if your memory was coming back. This actually makes my job easier. Where's the gold?"

"What gold? I don't know what you're talking about," Matthew insisted.

"The gold bars you found at the munitions dump in Syria." Gabe tilted his head. "When you fell through the floor in that back room."

Elizabeth didn't remember anything about any gold on the mission either. Hole? What the hell was Gabe talking about?

"Gabe, some of my memory is coming back, but I'm still missing huge chunks. I don't remember anything about that mission. Not a single fucking thing. I certainly don't know anything about any gold."

"Well, if you didn't move the gold then who did? I went back to get it about a month later and it was gone. I tore up that whole fucking floor, and every bar of gold was gone. You had disappeared for days after the explosion, so you had plenty of time to move all those gold bars. Are they still in that little village?" Gabe looked at Matt expecting an answer.

"I have absolutely no idea what the hell you're talking about." Matt's voice was now pleading. "I told you, only bits and pieces of my memory are coming back."

"Yeah, and it's too soon." Gabe paced the few feet, never dropping his gaze or the gun. He ran the fingers of his free hand through his hair "Everything got fucked up that day. You weren't even supposed to be there, Mason. You were supposed to be chasing a ghost forty miles away. The building was supposed to bury the fucking bars until we were ready to use it. No one was supposed to get hurt. A quick in, blow the building, and get the fuck out of there."

Gabe glared at Matthew. "But you saw the gold buried in the floor and like a fucking Boy Scout, tried to report it. Thank Allah we were the only ones who were listening live to the mission. I was ordered to kill you. But you didn't die there like you should have." Gabe screamed the last sentence.

"No. The mighty Mason Sinclair somehow made it out. Then those Goddamn SEALs rescued you. At that point, we had to keep you alive." His chuckle was maniacal. "But Mason Sinclair could die and had to."

"So that's when you created Matthew St. Clare?" Elizabeth clarified. "Why keep him alive?"

"Because he's the only one who knows where the gold is now." Gabe growled.

"Correction. I don't know where any gold is hidden," Matthew insisted. "I'll say it again, I don't remember anything about that mission. Maybe someday it'll come back, but not so far."

"Well, you did have what they considered a traumatic brain injury." Gabe continued as though talking to himself. "You were pretty banged up from the explosion. The SEAL team's report claimed that locals found you about half a mile from the burned-out building."

"If I have the information you want, then why are you trying to kill Elizabeth?" Matthew's question was the one she really wanted to ask, but she was smart enough not to bring attention to herself.

Gabe looked at Matthew as though he were an idiot. "To stop her from doing exactly what happened. The shrink said that only certain deep emotions, like love for someone in your past, could break through the mental cap he embedded in your memory. Obviously, that day you saw her at headquarters cracked the cap." Gabriel shook his head. "I told him it was a bad idea to take you to the cemetery with me, but did he listen? Fuck no. He had to test you. He had to know if you recognized her. Fucking shrinks, can't do their fucking job, and they leave me to clean up their fucking mess."

Gabriel was losing control. Elizabeth never took her eyes off the man she'd once called a friend. Her job with the CIA was nothing more than another way he, or they, could control her. But who are *they*?

Gabe was silent for nearly a full minute. "If you didn't move the gold, then who did?" Another long minute ensued but the muzzle of the gun never moved away from Matthew and Elizabeth. As if it had just come to him, Gabe grumbled. "That fucking bastard. He double crossed me. Fuck!" His gaze then returned to Elizabeth who now stood beside Matthew. The gun came up, pointed at her head. "Elizabeth, I'm sor—"

Matthew threw her on the floor toward the couch following her down. He reached up underneath the couch and came out with two handguns. Shoving one in her belly, he rolled away with the other, separating them, making it harder to shoot them both.

Before Gabe could get off a shot, Matthew double tapped him in the head at the same time the living room window exploded.

Elizabeth automatically rolled toward the couch giving the flying glass shards her back. "Matthew!" She shrieked.

"Lizzie, stay down." Matthew screamed at her. "There was a third shot. There's another shooter in the yard."

"Matthew, are you okay?" Please, God, don't take him from me again. We've just found each other. She remembered a throw blanket on the back of the couch and carefully snaked her hand up to grab it. She pulled it down and tucked it behind her, then shoved any glass shards away as she rolled over.

Dark blood pooled around Gabriel's body. A pang of sorrow ran through her for the man she thought was her friend. He was going to kill her without a second thought. Her gaze swept the room, searching desperately for Matthew.

Glass tinkled as he swept it out of the way with a pillow that had been sitting on the nearby chair. "I'm coming, sweetheart. Don't move." He glanced toward the picture window where a light breeze blew through a three-foot gap. "The other shooter might still be out there so stay low." He looked at her, then over at their friend's body. "I'm pretty sure, though, Gabe was his target." He crawled up next to her and swept the glass away so they could lean their backs against the bottom of the couch. When he took her in his arms, she felt safe for the first time in days. "We're going to be okay, sweetheart."

She looked up at him and laid her lips on his. The kiss was reassuring on so many levels. Matthew was alive. Mason was alive. The man she loved was alive.

He got his cell phone out of his back pocket and stared at it. "I'm not sure who to call first." He chuckled sardonically. "Normally, my first call is to Gabe."

They both stared at the dead body six feet away.

"Who is his boss?" Elizabeth offered as an alternative.

"Noah Hennel, the director of operations." Matthew's face scrunched. "Not exactly my biggest fan. The feeling is mutual."

Elizabeth shrugged. "Call him."

Twenty minutes later, Elizabeth got to meet Operations Director Noah Hennel. There was something about him that seemed familiar, but perhaps they had met before or she had seen him in the halls at headquarters. She instantly pegged him as Middle Eastern with his dark brown skin and black curly hair. Although he had no discernible accent, she'd swear he came from Iraq, Iran, maybe even Syria. Over the last sixty years, the United States had taken in so many refugees from that war-torn area of the world. Perhaps he'd come as a child. It didn't matter. He could not hold such a position within the Central Intelligence Agency if he had not been vetted to the nth degree.

At the door, Director Hennel signaled to the men in the

large white van that had followed his black SUV down Matthew's driveway. "Senior Special Agent St. Clare, Special Agent Kamp." He nodded rather than shake hands. He stepped into the living room and glanced around before his gaze landed on Gabriel. "This was a terrorist attack directly on senior agents within the agency. We're going to handle this internally. No outside organizations are to be involved." He turned and barely nodded at the man who had taken up post at the front door.

His gaze swept the living room one more time stopping where Elizabeth and Matthew stood side-by-side. "I checked the video on the way over. Everything seems clear. Self-defense." His gaze dropped to the guns on the coffee table. "They'll have to take the weapon you used to shoot Director Davis, but since the other one wasn't discharged, you can keep it."

He turned his dark brown eyes on Elizabeth and raked his gaze over her loose T-shirt and tight yoga pants. A flash of disgust crossed his face before he was able to school it. "In my opinion, the threat to you, Agent Kamp, is over."

Once again, his gaze scanned the living room. "I have the team waiting outside. They will take care of everything here, including removing the unauthorized audiovisual equipment. I've approved the agency to purchase your house. It's our experience that it's better to remove the agent from a home where violent acts had been committed. We'll have your belongings packed and moved into storage. You're both officially on five days administrative leave."

The front door opened, and the previous guard filled the frame. Elizabeth could see men lined up behind him.

"I'm going to let them start in here while you pack your bags."

As they stepped into Matthew's bedroom and closed the door, he took her into his arms. She hadn't realized how much she needed his touch. "You never answered my question."

What question? Which question? When she looked up at him he smiled.

"Elizabeth Kamp, are you going to marry me or not?" He looked nervous, as though she might say no.

She cupped his face in both hands. "Who am I going to marry? Matthew St. Clare, or Mason Sinclair?"

He dropped his forehead the short distance to hers. "I think for now, I'd better remain Matthew St. Clare. Someone from the CIA ordered my brainwashing. I can't let anyone know that I'm regaining my memory. Can we keep that our secret for now?"

She completely understood why he wanted to keep up the façade of Matthew St. Clare. She tilted her head up and kissed his lips. "I would be honored to marry Matthew St. Clare."

He crashed his mouth on hers and deepened the kiss. She tangled her tongue with his, letting him know that she wanted him, now and forever. When they broke apart they were both breathing heavily. She glanced over at her still packed suitcases.

"Give me ten minutes to pack." He kissed her quickly. "Then let's go get our children."

CHAPTER NINETEEN

Fourteen Hours Later

"I hear you have been doing a little housecleaning lately." His uncle must have spies at the CIA. The thought that someone who worked for him may be reporting to his uncle, Nassar al-Jamil, infuriated the man behind the mahogany desk. How dare his uncle spy on him? He began to make a mental list of all possible spies, then nearly laughed out loud. The CIA was filled with spies for both sides. He just needed to ferret out which ones were reporting back to his uncle about *his* activities.

"I wouldn't call it housekeeping. I think of it as taking out the trash." The man picked up his favorite Mont Blanc pen from the marble desk set. Gabriel Davis had served his purpose for many years but he had also been a pain in his backside. He was never truly convinced of Gabe's dedication to their cause. His judgment had been in front of Allah.

"I will personally be taking over watching Matthew Saint Clare. I intend on promoting him to Director of Special

Activities Division." He chuckled as he played with his pen. "He won't have time to think about his past. Between his new wife, new house, children— and I heard rumors that he and Elizabeth were considering having more children."

"Having children is no big deal," his uncle scoffed. "I have at least twenty of them."

He chuckled. "You also have twelve wives. I don't have time to bother with even one wife."

"When you join me in the promised land, you can have as many as you wish." His uncles promise was tempting, but he still had a great deal of work to complete in the United States.

"Another reason I look forward to joining you." He added getting laid to his to do list for that night. He had a cache of several women who were more than willing to entertain him for a few hours before he left their bed. His powerful government position had served him well over the years.

"Are you sure Gabriel left no trace of what he did for us?" A hint of nervousness could be detected in his uncle's voice.

Once again, the man took it as a personal insult that his own family didn't trust him to do everything that needed to be done. "I'm positive," he said through clenched teeth. "I had my best team search his apartment immediately after they had killed him. He kept no records and always used the burner phone which has been destroyed."

"What of the others?"

I expect they'll show up for Gabriel's funeral and while they are together with Matthew and Elizabeth, I'll have someone on them. In all this time, they haven't put it together yet."

"Good. You know what to do if that happens." His uncle, again, telling him how to do his job as though he hadn't been doing it successfully for the past thirty years.

The man smacked the pen down on the desk. He didn't

need his uncle telling him how to do his job. "All three are being handled. The two in the military are neck deep in missions around the world. The woman is swimming as hard as she can, but her weakness is her mother. I know where that woman is every day and if I need to put my hands on her to bring Teagan to heel I will.

"How hard can it be to control her? She's just a woman." Disdain filled the man's voice half a world away.

"But uncle, she is an American woman, and they're very different than those in your country," he reminded the older man. "Women here have a mind of their own. They can do what they want without a man's permission."

"This is exactly why Allah has chosen me to create the New Islamic State."

Before his uncle started to rant, the man in the executive office at Langley slid over a piece of paper. "Tell me, uncle, what is it that we need to build your army of Allah?" He pulled up all the current missions around the world and look at the inventory that could possibly be retrieved.

"Are you growing your own stockpile?" His uncle asked. "It will not be long before we will bring the United States to its knees once again."

Of all the things he had personally done or ordered, the camps in Pennsylvania, Kansas, and Washington state were the only ones that could get him tried for treason. He'd be long gone from his beautiful Georgetown home before he could even be arrested. The hidden stack of passports, duffel bag of cash, and go bag were always within reach. The CIA had taught him well.

CHAPTER TWENTY

Two days later, Matthew and Elizabeth sat at the dining room table in the residential hotel shuffling the sales sheets of the homes they had looked at that day. Elizabeth did not want them to live in the home she had shared with Robert and returning to his home was impossible.

Lizzie tapped her manicured nail on a house he considered his favorite. "I really like this one. It has a great backyard for the kids, in an awesome school district, it's only an extra ten minutes for each of us to work, and I really like that huge family room."

"Then that's the one." He leaned over and kissed her. She immediately wrapped her arms around his neck and took the kiss deep, the way he liked it. He thrust his tongue inside her mouth and got lost in the promise of later that night.

"Yuck," Austin said as he emerged from the second bedroom. "Do I have to see you two kiss all the time now that you're married?"

They broke apart and laughed. Three days ago, they had opted for another quick courthouse ceremony. Neither had wanted to wait another day. After a few hours of slow, passionate lovemaking in their bed at their temporary lodging, they had gone to pick up the children and announced their wedding.

Matthew had been so nervous, especially about the way Austin would take the news. To his and Lizzie's surprise, the boy had remarked, "About time. Glad you found a good one this time, Mom." He then hugged his mother. "Can we celebrate with pizza? I'm starved." He then looked Matthew in the eyes and asked, "Can I get my own spicy sausage pizza, Dad? I really hate the ham and pineapple they eat." He jabbed his thumb toward his mother and Liza.

All the air had left Matthew's lungs. His son had called him Dad. "Sure, son." He choked out.

Liza had raised her arms. "Up, please, Daddy."

He had to suck in a breath before he grabbed his little girl. His baby girl.

Planted on his hip, she put both tiny hands on his cheeks and drew his face to within an inch of his. "You're my real dad now, right? You're going to take me to the zoo, and to the Children's Museum so I can climb the wall 'cause they have a special one for kids my age, and we're gonna go to the beach and build sand castles, and when it snows we're going to build a snowman, and you're going to build me a swing, and maybe a fort just for girls." Finally stopping, she glared at her brother. "And no boys allowed."

Matthew couldn't hold back a smile. "So, is that what real daddies do?"

Liza nodded. "My friend, Ginny, said that's what she and her real dad do. He comes and gets her sometimes on the weekend and they go have fun. Real dads are 'posed to be fun." Her face went white and her chin quivered.

"What's the matter, sweetheart?" He wondered how he had already screwed up fatherhood.

She blinked back tears and shook her head. "I don't want

you to go away during the week. You don't have to take me to special places and only come get me on weekends. You can stay all the time. Mommy has a big bed and you can sleep in her room." The child put her soft hands around Matthew's ear and whispered loudly. "Mommy's a good snuggler, 'specially when it thunders."

"Pretty sure he was going to sleep there anyway, little sis." Austin gave him a knowing smile. For a nine-year-old, his son seemed to be quite mature. Matthew suddenly worried about having *the talk*. He couldn't remember when his father had taken him into his office on the backside of their sprawling ranch home and handed him his first box of condoms, but he was relatively sure he'd reached his teens.

Liza had insisted on calling the Sinclair's and sharing their news. His father had seemed overly friendly, happy about the marriage. He overheard his mother telling Elizabeth that she had a good feeling about this one. Someday, hopefully soon, his parents were in for a big surprise when they revealed his real identity. Until then, Matthew hated pretending, but it was to keep everyone he loved safe.

"Yep. We're going to be kissing all the time." Lizzie unwound herself from him bringing him back to the present.

"Sorry, son, you just have to get used to it." Matt loved calling Austin his son. They hadn't told him yet and wouldn't until the time was right, when they were completely out of danger.

"If you two are going to keep kissing, I'm gonna go kill aliens on my videogame." The boy grabbed a can of soda and disappeared back down the hall.

Matthew's phone alerted that someone was coming down the hallway toward their suite. He checked the video on his cell and saw it was Teagan. Flipping the live shot to Elizabeth, she rose to greet her friend at the door.

After hugs, the two made their way back to the dining room.

"You are never going to believe what my friend found," Teagan started.

Matthew took one look at the armload of papers and hoped it was good news.

Teagan started pulling out stacks held with huge black clips. "Well, Elizabeth, your former husband took a second mortgage on your house so he could buy timeshares in the Caribbean. Now this isn't just any old timeshare, this is an all-inclusive, high end, multi-resort."

"Great, I now own a timeshare." Elizabeth certainly didn't sound excited.

Teagan giggled. "Oh, no. You own three of them. It seems every time he used one of his weeks, he took a different woman to each resort. According to my friend, Robert gave each one of them the Honeymoon Experience as they named it. When they returned to the United States, he would dump them. He told each woman the same story, that he realized he loved his wife and couldn't see her anymore."

Matthew could tell by the look on Elizabeth's face she was not impressed. In fact, she was pissed. "Is that all he found?"

"Sorry, but no." Teagan picked up another piece of paper. "Each time, he had paid his credit card off quickly after one of those trips. He had spent a great deal of money on the women. They would go snorkeling, have private dinners on a catamaran sunset cruise, on one trip Robert and his friend learned to scuba dive, and after that he went often."

"I'm an idiot," Elizabeth admitted. "I guess I should've noticed when he came back with a tan after attending a week-long conference. "The last credit card bill was nearly ten thousand dollars. Where did it all go?"

Teagan smiled. "You may live a frugal life, but your

husband certainly didn't. First-class tickets for two at the last-minute cost about a thousand each. And remember, I told you these are high-end resorts. Even though they're all-inclusive, they have specialty restaurants. Personally, I can't imagine any Chinese meal worth a hundred and fifty dollars per person, but your husband's last girlfriend liked eating there. I mentioned that sunset cruise, Robert bought out the boat so they could have the catamaran all to themselves. That was a mere fifteen hundred dollars."

Elizabeth's mouth dropped open. "He didn't even want to go to the Maryland Eastern Shore with me and the kids and stay in a condo, so I never booked the trip. How dare he complain about the cost. I guess sand and sun with me and the kids couldn't compare to the vacation he was giving his girlfriends."

Teagan nodded "And Robert was doing this three times a year."

"Is there any chance I can sell these things and get some of the money back?" Lizzie still owed several thousand on the second mortgage and the credit cards Robert had left her to pay.

"You can get the money back from the most recent one he purchased." Teagan shrugged. "There's a possibility that you might be able to get some money back by selling one of them but don't be surprised if you only get pennies on the dollar. You're competing against the sales company that flies in dozens of unsuspecting couples every week when you try to sell one of these timeshares. Most likely, you'll be stuck with at least one of them." Teagan smiled. "A week in the Caribbean in January when it's cold and slushy here in DC sounds pretty damn good to me."

"Me too," Matthew commented. "Please tell me these resorts aren't adults only." He was really hoping they weren't the kind of places where people in the BDSM lifestyle vacationed. That would shock Lizzie even more to discover Robert had been into that kind of sex.

Teagan shuffled through some papers and pulled out a colorful brochure. "Nope. The one in Cancún, and another on St. Kitts, have Kids' Clubs on the property, but Robert never went to either of those two. I'm sure we'll find even more that are kid friendly."

Matthew hugged his wife. "Looks like we're taking our honeymoon in the Caribbean and bringing the kids with us."

Teagan's eyes got big. "Honeymoon?" She shrieked and grabbed Lizzie's hand. She stared at the original diamond and wedding band Matthew had bought for her ten years ago. She had kept it for Austin to give to his fiancée someday. He also wore his original ring that Elizabeth had discovered when Matthew's affects had been returned to her after his supposed death.

Teagan looked back and forth between Matthew and Elizabeth. "You two got married? When?"

"Yesterday." Lizzie held out her free hand and pulled Matthew in close. Her smile beamed with love.

"You went off and got married without me, again." Teagan hugged Elizabeth and when she stepped back she looked guilty, like she'd said more than she should have.

Lizzie gave her a reassuring smile. "Don't worry, Matthew knows all about Mason. Well, almost everything." When she looked up at him, she had questions in her eyes.

They had agreed to tell no one that Matthew and Mason were the same person and his memories were returning more and more every day. Until they could figure out who had shot Gabe with a sniper rifle from Matthew's backyard, and what gold their former friend had been talking about, that subject was going to have to remain their secret.

Austin and Liza came running into the room. "Aunt

Teagan, guess what?" Liza through her arms around Teagan's waist.

She immediately picked up the little girl and popped Liza onto her hip. "What are you all fired excited about?" Teagan's love for the child was unmistakable. He and Lizzie had discussed their friends desire for children, but between her mother's failing health and the lack of a constant man in her life, that opportunity had passed her.

"Matthew is our new daddy and he's going to make it 'fficial. We're going to get 'dopted so I'm not going to be Elizabeth Ann Vetatucci anymore, I'm going to be Elizabeth Ann Saint Clare, but I'm still going to be called Liza." The precious child who was soon-to-be his legal daughter finally took a breath.

Austin sidled up next to him and Matthew automatically put his arm around the boy's shoulders. He'd swear his son grew more each day, but perhaps it was just that he was standing up straight and tall now that Robert was out of his life. He'd seen a significant difference in the boy's attitude in just a few short weeks they'd been together almost constantly.

"So, Austin, what did you think about all this?" Teagan asked.

"I'm okay with it." The huge smile on his face and the way he put his arm around Matthew's waist said so much more.

"Exactly when were you going to tell me about this?" Teagan looked accusingly at Elizabeth.

"We didn't want to say anything until after...Gabe's funeral." Lizzie winced. She was still having a difficult time reconciling that the man she had known for years, thought of as a good friend, had held her at gunpoint and tried to kill her. They were both working through those emotions while attempting to put the puzzle pieces together in a way that made sense.

"As soon as we get settled into a new house, we were going to have you, Logan, and Micah over for dinner." Matthew had hoped to find out more about what happened at the Syrian ammunitions dump from the other two men. Very little of that time had come back to him. That explosion was the pivotal point in everything that had happened, including Gabe's death. Matthew still had a difficult time believing that Gabriel was not truly his friend these past ten years. There was more to the situation than either he or Lizzie knew. Somehow, Teagan, Logan, and Micah were also involved. It may take months or years, but Matthew would get to the bottom of it.

In the meantime, Matthew was determined to make up for the ten years he missed with his son and wife, and to make a new life filled with love for all of them.

Be sure to look for Book #2 in the Never Forgotten trilogy, A Promise Never Forgotten. Teagan and Logan's story will be available at all e-book retailers in February 2019.

If you've enjoyed ***A Love Never Forgotten***, please tell others what you liked about this book by leaving a review on your retailer's site.

Consider other books by KaLyn Cooper:

Click on the titles to learn more and for BUY links.

ALSO BY KALYN COOPER

Black Swan Series

Unconventional Beginnings: Prequel (Black Swan Novella # 0.5)

Unrelenting Love: **Lady Hawk (Katlin) & Alex** (Black Swan Book #1)

Noel's Puppy Power: **Bailey & Tanner** *(*A Sweet Christmas Black Swan Novella #1.5)

Uncaged Love: **Harper & Rafe** (Black Swan Book #2)

Unexpected Love: **Lady Eagle (Grace) & Griffin** (Black Swan Book #3)

Challenging Love: **Katlin & Alex** *(*A Black Swan Novella #3.5)

Unguarded Love: **Lady Harrier (Nita) & Daniel** (Black Swan Book #4)

Choosing Love: **Grace & Griffin** *(*A Black Swan Novella #4.5)

Guardian Elite Series

Double Jeopardy (Novella #2 Guardian Elite series crossover with Hildie McQueen's Indulgences series)

Justice for Gwen (Novella #2 Guardian Elite series crossover with Susan Stoker's Special Forces World)

Rescuing Melina (Novella #3 Guardian Elite series crossover with Susan Stoker's Special Forces World)

Snow SEAL (Novella #4 Guardian Elite series crossover with Elle James Brotherhood Protectors World)

Cancun Series

Christmas in Cancun (Cancun Series Book #1)

Conquered in Cancun (Cancun Series Novella #1.5)

Captivated in Cancun (Cancun Series Book #2)

Claimed by a SEAL (Cancun Series crossover Novella #2.5)

Crisis in Cancun (Cancun Series Book #3)

Never Forgotten Trilogy

A Love Never Forgotten

A Promise Never Forgotten - Releasing February 2019.

ABOUT THE AUTHOR

USA Today Bestselling author KaLyn Cooper writes romantic suspense based in fact. Twenty seven years as a military wife has shown her the world and the men and women who protect it every day. Thirty years in PR taught her fact can be stranger than fiction, but she leaves it up to the reader to separate truth from imagination. She and her husband live in Tennessee on their micro-plantation filled with gardens, cattle, quail, and a bird dog. When she's not writing, she's at the shooting range or paddling on the river.

Contact KaLyn

For all the latest info, check out **KaLyn's website**
www.KaLynCooper.com

Sign up for exclusive promotions and special offers only available in **KaLyn's newsletter**
http://www.kalyncooper.com/newsletter.html
Email: KaLyn@KaLynCooper.com

facebook.com/kalyn.cooper.52
twitter.com/KaLynCooperbooks
instagram.com/kalyncooper
bookbub.com/authors/kalyn-cooper

Printed in Great Britain
by Amazon